Also by Ruth Cardello

Lone Star Burn

Taken, Not Spurred

Tycoon Takedown

The Legacy Collection

Maid for the Billionaire

For Love or Legacy

Bedding the Billionaire

Saving the Sheikh

Rise of the Billionaire

Breaching the Billionaire: Alethea's Redemption

The Andrades

Come Away with Me

Home to Me

Maximum Risk

Somewhere Along the Way

Loving Gigi

The Barrington Billionaires

Always Mine

Stolen Kisses

LONE STAR BURN

Taken Home

RUTH CARDELLO

Montlake
Romance

Published by Montlake Romance, Seattle

www.apub.com

Amazon, the Amazon logo, and Montlake Romance are trademarks of Amazon.com, Inc., or its affiliates.

ISBN-13: 9781503934665
ISBN-10: 1503934667

Cover design by Kerrie Robertson

Printed in the United States of America

To my parents, who are both gone now, for instilling in me a belief in family and forgiveness. It's impossible to have one without the other.

Chapter One

Don't panic. It's just a wedding. Chelle Landon held her bouquet of flowers tightly against the front of her ill-fitting bridesmaid dress. Her mother had suggested she get the bodice taken in, but Chelle was in denial. Who wants to go to the seamstress and say, "Smaller. Smaller. No, even smaller than that"? She might not be flat-chested, but she didn't have what the strapless dress had been designed to cling to.

She turned away from the people who had filled Fort Mavis's small church to the brim and tugged one side of the dress up. *I should have worn that padded strapless bra my mother suggested. But no, I had to choose a lace demi because I wanted to feel sexy.* She shifted again and tugged at the other side of the bodice. *Instead, I feel like a five-year-old playing dress-up.*

She was lucky to be part of this bridal party. Horse trainer Tony Carlton was famous in Texas, and his northerner soon-to-be wife, Sarah Dery, was a beloved addition to the area. As one of their closest neighbors, Chelle had been a natural choice of friend. She and Sarah went to lunch at least once a week. It was not only a privilege to be in the wedding, it was also a pleasure.

Or so she kept telling herself.

The wedding was making her face her love life—or lack of one. Chelle glanced around the small church. At the end of the ceremony, the pool of single men would officially be down another man.

Chelle looked the happy couple over again. It wasn't that she wanted Tony or that she thought he belonged with someone else. Anyone who spent five minutes with the couple could see how happy they were. It was simply the idea of there being one less opportunity in a town that was beginning to suffocate her.

Beside Tony was the best man, Charles Dery: rich, gorgeous, and paired with his fiancée and the maid of honor, Melanie Hanna. Tony's brother, Dean, was paired with Lucy, one of the bride's friends from college. He was attractive and only a couple of years older than Chelle, but they had gone on one date when he'd moved to the area, and there hadn't been a spark.

Height-wise, Chelle should have been paired with Dean, but that would have put David with Lucy, and no one wanted that. Not after Lucy had broken David's heart and gotten engaged to someone else, or so the gossip mill claimed. Chelle hadn't wanted to pin Sarah down on the subject so close to her wedding. Thus, David and Chelle rounded out the bridal party.

David Harmon. A respectable choice with a reputation for being a man of good character. Any woman would be lucky to land him. Sadly, Chelle had never felt anything for him, either.

Chelle snuck a look at the people in attendance again, and Bobby Mulner winked at her. She shot him a small smile and looked away. If she hadn't grown up with him, he wouldn't be a bad choice. He owned a trucking business and was slowly buying up land in the area in preparation for diversifying his company.

At least, that's what he'd told her the last time he'd asked her out. It hadn't changed her answer, though. All she could see when she looked at him was the snot collection he'd kept in his desk in fourth grade.

Chelle shuddered at the memory.

I need to get out of this town.

Men were out there. Single, wonderful men. Melanie was proof that leaving Fort Mavis brought new and wonderful opportunities.

I don't even need a fiancé. At this point, I'd take one hot romp. Who knew that her decision to wait until her wedding night to have sex would have brought her here, to a place full of regret, not for what she had done but for what she hadn't? She considered saying yes to Bobby, just to get it over with, but she wasn't that desperate yet. *Is it wrong to want more? To think I should feel something when I look into a man's eyes?*

I didn't know virginity had an expiration date. Good until . . . oh my God, if I turn twenty-six and haven't slept with anyone, the man I finally do have sex with will think I'm a freak.

After a certain age, having had sex, even too much, sounds better than trying to explain why you've never taken the plunge—so to speak. Men saw it as a problem, a symptom of something, rather than the culmination of a strict upbringing and a shallow pool of choices.

And it's not an ailment I can discuss with anyone. Chronic chastity. The most blatant symptom? Envying Ava Edwards, who slept with half the guys in high school, because even she is married now.

Chelle felt a mild panic set in as the minister had Sarah and Tony repeat their vows. *I am standing next to the only other women in my age group in Fort Mavis who are single, and they are both engaged.*

Slow down, everyone. I need a little more time.

"If anyone here knows a reason why these two cannot wed, speak now or forever hold your peace," the minister said, looking up from the couple for a moment.

"I do," Chelle said to herself, not realizing that her voice would carry in the silence of the church.

Everyone, including the bride and groom, turned to Chelle in shock. If death could come from embarrassment, Chelle would have died on the spot. With her cheeks burning red, she glanced at the people seated in the church pews and met the deep-blue eyes of a man standing in the back of the church. He arched one eyebrow in response to her sustained gaze.

An entirely different kind of heat spread through her. He was tall, with broad shoulders that his dark suit accentuated rather than concealed. His blond hair was long enough to have a boyish curl to it, but there was nothing boyish about him. No, he was all man and, even if just for that moment, his attention was all hers.

Tan like most of the men Chelle knew, but not with the toughened look ranchers had, this man was smooth, polished, and hotter than hell. He shot her a cocky grin that told her he knew exactly what she was thinking—and liked it.

Conceited bastard. Chelle licked her lips nervously. *But oh so attractive.*

As if he'd heard her thoughts, his smile widened, and Chelle nearly passed out from the beauty of it. No one like him had ever come through her town. He belonged in a painting or on a movie screen. *But who is he?* She'd heard that Charles had famous friends. Could he be one of them?

He'd be the kind of mistake a woman would smile about later, regardless of how their time together ended.

She closed her eyes and thought, *If you're listening, God, please forgive me for what I'm imagining doing with him.* She opened her eyes and felt another wave of desire flood her. *Unless you sent him for me, and then thank you.*

The minister cleared his throat, then coughed loudly, and the sound pulled Chelle's attention reluctantly away from the physical manifestation of her late-night fantasies. Tony and Sarah were looking at her with awkward intensity. In fact, everyone was staring at her.

It was only then that she remembered what she'd said aloud. She smiled sheepishly and waved her flowers in the air in a cheerlike move. "I mean, I do believe they should be together forever. Yay for them," she ended and squared her shoulders. With that action, the bodice of her dress slipped down an inch, revealing the top of her lace bra. Chelle yanked it back up and turned to once again face Sarah and Tony with silent respect.

Once the minister began speaking again, Chelle snuck another glance at the man standing in the back of the church. He had his arms folded across his chest, and his eyes danced with amusement.

Suddenly, being the only single woman left in Fort Mavis was not such a bad thing.

Son of a bitch. I guess it has to be her.

Mason Thorne hoped that, despite her humorous display a moment ago, she could keep a straight face long enough to pose for a photo or two with him, or more if that was what was required. He was willing to pay her for her time. According to the ushers, the still-blushing bridesmaid with the dress she couldn't keep on was the only single woman at the wedding.

She was a petite thing, slender with the kind of wholesome long dark-blonde hair that couldn't be replicated in a salon. He guessed her to be in her midtwenties. Every inch of her was adorable.

But she wasn't his type. That would make this ruse easier. He preferred women bold like a good whiskey or easy on the palate like his favorite beer. Chelle Landon looked sweet and way too innocent for his taste.

Mason prided himself on having good instincts when it came to women. On any other day, Mason would have said he loved women in general. Loved the way they smelled, the sounds they made during sex.

He'd heard men say women were all the same. Those men were idiots, and they were missing out without even knowing it. Exploring the nuances of what drove one woman wild or left her cold was fascinating. *Colleges should offer that as an elective.*

Mason didn't feel guilty about his long list of partners. They weren't conquests. He never understood men who needed to prove themselves by chasing and dominating women. To him, it was like bragging about putting a leash on a puppy. If a man understood women at all, he could have them following him around, begging for sex.

That was the power of a mind-blowing orgasm. Although sometimes it could be too powerful. Trish Shugarts should have been a one-night stand.

Mason had met her at a movie premiere. They'd both had a little too much to drink, and she'd offered to go home with him. The sex that night had been mediocre at best. He'd never been one to leave a woman less than satisfied, though. So in the morning, he'd taken his time and made her come until all she could do was smile at him gratefully.

As they say, no good deed goes unpunished.

He hadn't realized she was the daughter of Senator Bill Shugarts, a man who was already hell-bent on opposing any bill Mason put forth out of spite. How was Mason supposed to recognize a daughter Shugarts never took to any events? Politics was a dirty sport, though, and enemies were easy enough to come by. Shugarts would see Mason's slipup as a deliberate move against his family. The level of emotion Shugarts would likely bring to every encounter outweighed the annoyance of what Mason was about to do.

Trish had called him the next day. She'd quickly revealed symptoms of the dreaded NBSNT (Never Been Said No To) syndrome that afflicted many daughters of rich men. She'd wanted to see him again, and when he'd refused, it had been as if a switch had flipped in her head. She'd gone from adoring to threatening to tell her father.

Damn my talented tongue and possessive women.

He didn't like to lie, but not every situation benefited from the truth. In a moment of inspiration, he'd played the female-solidarity card and told her he was in a relationship and trying to change his ways. He'd said straying had been a huge mistake, one he was eaten with guilt over. All he could do, he'd said, was grovel for his girlfriend's forgiveness and hope she stayed with him.

"What's her name?" Trish had asked keenly.

"I'd rather not say," Mason had said. "We've kept our relationship low profile for her protection. You know how the press is."

"Everyone knows you don't believe in relationships."

Mason had held to his lie. Strong people could be intimidated. Crooked people could be forced to right their ways. But crazy? Crazy people played by their own rules and were best steered clear of. "Love changes everyone."

If that had been enough to deter Trish, Mason wouldn't have been late to the wedding. But she'd followed him to the airport and accused him of lying to her. She'd wanted to come with him, but he'd told her he was going to a wedding in Texas with his girlfriend.

"You? In love? I won't believe that until I see it," Trish had said.

Oh, you'll see it. I'll bring back the damn bridesmaid herself if I have to. I am not starting World War III with Shugarts because his daughter thinks I should be her bedside vibrator.

But I wish Chelle looked a little less eager. This is complicated enough. I don't want to shed one problem and gain another.

He gave the adorably awkward bridesmaid another once-over, then smiled at her. She looked like a reasonable person. If he explained the situation to her, she might even enjoy helping him out.

He watched her tug at her drooping bodice again, and his cock twitched with interest. He reminded himself harshly, *This is not about sex. This is damage control.*

Chapter Two

At the end of the ceremony, Chelle linked arms with David, and together they followed the other couples and the bride and groom down the aisle. Tension stood out in David's normally relaxed face. Chelle tugged on his arm. He leaned in, and she said, "Is it awful having Lucy in the bridal party, too?"

His expression went deliberately blank. "No reason why it should be."

"I heard you and she—"

"You heard wrong," David said firmly and raised his head.

"I'm sorry," Chelle said. The last thing she wanted to do was to make David feel worse than he probably already did.

He laid his hand over hers on his arm. "Things work out the way they're meant to, Chelle."

Chelle's attention darted to the blond man who was still standing in the back of the church. *You mean like a beautiful man showing up just when I'd resigned myself to possibly dying a virgin?* Chelle held in the thought. She couldn't imagine what David's reaction would have been if she'd shared it. Instead, she asked, "David, who is that man standing in the back?"

David followed her gaze and made a face. "California State Senator Mason Thorne. He's a friend of Charles's."

Keeping her voice down as they approached him, Chelle asked, "Is he single?"

David frowned. "Steer clear of that one, Chelle. He's a player. He went from being a movie star to a politician. Men like that have egos the size of Texas. He'll only be looking for one thing when he comes alone to a wedding."

Oh, I hope so. Chelle craned her neck to catch one last look at the state senator before walking out of the main part of the church and into the foyer. She pieced together what she'd heard about Mason from Sarah and Melanie. He'd started off as a child star, had some blockbusters that made him a household name, then walked away from that career. Although all of that was fascinating, it didn't compare to how she'd felt when she'd looked at him. She'd finally felt that spark she'd been holding out for. *He's alone. I'm alone.* "I'll be careful," Chelle promised. *Well, not too careful. I can't let an opportunity like this pass me by. If Ava Edwards could sleep with most of the football team, surely I can have one wild night and not regret it. Would a man like that bring a condom?*

Oh my God, am I honestly thinking about sleeping with a man I don't even know?

Yes.

Please, yes.

It's time to stop waiting and start living.

Carefully. I don't want to go through what Melanie did.

So I hope he brought protection with him.

That's not good enough. People make their own fate.

I need a condom.

The problem with living in a small town was that if she walked into a pharmacy and purchased any type of birth control, her phone would be ringing within minutes, and it would likely be her mother asking who she was intending to do the deed with. *Hell, by now she'd probably be relieved.*

Like dating, her options when it came to getting what she wanted were limited. She could hope the senator traveled with one, or she could ask Melanie or Sarah if they had one. No, if she did that, she'd be forced to answer a slew of questions she didn't want to consider the answers to. Like "Is this a wise course of action?"

Whoever she asked had to be discreet. Someone who wouldn't want the details. Someone like David. As they stood on the stairs of the church together, waiting for instructions on where to go for the photo session, Chelle tugged on David's arm again. He inclined his head to hear her. "Do you have a condom?" she asked softly.

His head snapped around, and he met her eyes. "A what?"

The photographer asked them to stand and pose. Chelle faced forward with her best photogenic smile and said through her teeth, "You heard me. I don't want to explain myself. Either you have one or you don't. You can give it to me or not, but let's not talk about it."

The photographer moved on to take a photo of Melanie with Charles. Chelle shook her head in disappointment. It was probably too much to expect a man like David to have one.

Chelle felt something pressed into her hand. She looked down, and a huge smile spread across her face. She tucked the condom into the side of her lace bra, then went up onto her tiptoes and gave David a kiss on the cheek. "If I was at all attracted to you—" She stopped herself there when she thought about how that sounded. "You know what I mean."

David chuckled. "I do. Just be careful."

Chelle glanced over her shoulder and saw Mason watching her from just outside the church door. She turned away with a smile she was sure was even brighter than before. *I don't want to be careful. I want to be spontaneous for once. And tonight I'm going to be.*

For the next hour, the bridal party was shuffled around the church steps and lawn for individual and group photos. The day was getting warmer, but Chelle didn't mind. She felt like she floated from one shot to the next. All she could think about was the man who looked like he was waiting for her to finish.

Near the end of the session, the photographer asked if he could take one more shot of her alone. She posed beside a tree and looked over the photographer's shoulder to see if Mason was still on the church steps. He was. Their eyes met briefly, and Chelle's libido went into overdrive. *How could I feel this good when we haven't done more than look at each other?*

"Have you ever thought of modeling?" the photographer asked. "You have a presence that's truly captivating. An expression that could sell anything. I can't quite describe it, but it's beautiful."

"Thank you," Chelle said with a smile that could not be suppressed. Although she dreamed of doing something outside of helping her parents run their ranch, she was realistic about her looks. She also knew exactly what the man could likely see in her eyes. She'd never been as excited about anything as she was about testing whether or not kissing Senator Thorne could possibly feel as good as she imagined. "I have to go."

On any other day, Chelle would have played harder to get. She would have pretended not to notice how Mason was watching her as if she were his prey for the evening. That day, however, she wanted there to be zero chance of him losing interest and moving on. A man that hot could tempt a few of the married women to consider bending their vows a bit, and that was not a risk she was willing to take.

She hiked up the bodice of her dress and walked up the church steps to where Mason was standing. She didn't stop until she was about a foot in front of him. Even leaning against the outside wall of the church, he was gloriously tall, which forced her to tip her head back to look up at him. "Hi," she said breathlessly. "My name is Chelle Landon."

The smile he gave her had her innards quivering with desire. He straightened, looming even higher above her. She stared into his blue eyes, wondering if there was anything more beautiful on the whole planet. "I know," he said in a deep voice that exceeded her fantasy of how sexy he would sound. He held out his hand. "I'm Mason Thorne."

His strong hand swallowed Chelle's small one. That simple touch sent her imagination running with how his hands would feel on other parts of her body. *Wow. So this is what it's supposed to feel like. This is desire.* She shook his hand forcefully—longer than she meant to, but only realizing it when he looked down at their hands. "Sorry," she said and broke their connection. "We don't get many new people in Fort Mavis. I'm so used to knowing everyone."

Mason gave her a charming smile. "Then that gives you an advantage today. I hardly know anyone. It's a pleasure to meet you."

"The pleasure's mine," Chelle said quickly. *At least I hope it will be. Stop. Don't ruin this by sounding like an idiot. Try to look cool.* "I have to ride to the reception with the wedding party, but Sarah said the seats aren't assigned for dinner, so maybe we could sit together. I'd love to hear what you think of Fort Mavis." *Or anything.*

"I'd like that." He looked down at her for a long moment with an expression Chelle couldn't decipher. "I have something I'd like to ask you, but we can discuss it later when we have more time."

Chelle heard Melanie calling for her. It wasn't easy, but she tore her eyes away from Mason and turned. The rest of the wedding party was waiting beside the limo. "I have to go."

"I'll save a seat for you at the reception."

Unable to think of an intelligent response, Chelle merely nodded and darted down the steps toward the limo. *Something he wants to ask me.* That was blunt, but maybe that's how people from the city were. Direct with what they wanted. It didn't matter, really. He'd be gone by the next day anyway. Why waste the evening pretending they didn't both want the same thing?

David was at the limo, holding the door open for her. Their eyes met briefly, and she said, "Don't say it, or I'll ask about Lucy again."

Message sent and received. David nodded, and Chelle slid inside the limo beside Melanie.

As they pulled out, Melanie turned to Chelle and in a low voice said, "I saw you talking to Charles's friend Mason. I don't like to say anything bad about anyone, and he's a good friend to Charles, but you need to be careful. He goes through women like some people go through bottles of water. He'll flirt and flatter you, but it doesn't mean anything."

Chelle smoothed the skirt of her dress and crossed her ankles. "I appreciate the warning."

Melanie pursed her lips, then said, "I just don't want to see you get hurt."

"I can take care of myself, thank you." Being wanted by a man like Mason, even if it didn't turn into anything serious, wouldn't hurt nearly as much as not being wanted by him. Had she and Melanie been alone, Chelle might have even explained that to her. Melanie had spent enough years on her own before meeting Charles that she would understand. Instead, she changed the subject to a topic she knew would distract Melanie. "Jace looked like a little man when I saw him standing next to Charles. They get on well, don't they? Is he riding over with your parents?"

Melanie's eyes misted, and she linked her hand with Charles's. "He's growing up so fast. I used to worry that I hadn't done right by him, but he has good men in his life, and that will make all the difference. Charles is going to make a great father." She turned to the other two men in the limo. "I am really lucky. David, Jace wouldn't be nearly the kind soul he is if it weren't for you. And Dean, he wouldn't be grounded as often if you hadn't shared your childhood stories with him."

Dean smiled shamelessly. "A boy has to get his wild out while he's young, or he'll spend the rest of his life trying to hold it in."

Chelle laughed. "That doesn't sound like advice a sheriff should give. Does the same apply to girls?"

Even though there wasn't an ounce of attraction between them, Dean was fun to flirt with. He winked at her. "You tell me, darlin'."

Chelle blushed deeply, looked out the limo window, and whispered to herself, "Oh yes. Yes it does."

Seated at a table in a small reception hall in what appeared to be the nicest hotel in the area, Mason downed his drink, then told himself to go easy. He was irritated with himself for the way his cock had come to life while he watched Chelle posing for the wedding photos. There was something about her, something he couldn't look away from, and he didn't like it. Not one bit.

She didn't seem like someone who would understand that sex could occur with no commitment. Which was a problem. She also found him attractive. Another problem. And then there were the unsettling feelings that had coursed through him when she'd kissed David on the cheek. He'd wanted to walk over and demand she stop. *Ridiculous. I'm not the jealous type, and she means nothing to me.* He looked down at the ice in the bottom of his glass, then pushed the glass away. *I should stop drinking before I accidentally sleep with her.*

The music changed, and a man asked everyone to stand while the bridal party entered the room. Due to his height, Mason was easily able to watch them walk in. *Damn.* People said brides glowed, but Chelle positively beamed, even in her secondary role. Her eyes met his, and he felt the connection like a punch that sent him rocking back onto his heels. He attributed the sensation to the liquor he'd imbibed.

The bridal party stood off to one side as the bride and groom danced, then they paired up and joined them. Once they'd all been dancing for a while, the DJ asked the onlookers to please sit. Mason did so gladly. He was done watching Chelle laugh as David swung her around the dance floor.

Mason introduced himself to the people at his table. They asked him a hundred questions, sending his head spinning, making him feel as if he were being interviewed. He must have missed the song ending, because he wasn't aware Chelle was at his side until he heard her voice.

"May I join you?" Chelle asked.

Mason instantly stood and pulled out the chair beside him. "Of course. I saved a seat for you."

She gave him a look from beneath her long lashes that sent his heart racing. "Thank you."

She took the seat beside him, and he sat down once again, chastising himself silently. *Don't be a fool. This is not the time, nor is she the woman, for what you're thinking.*

After a short pause, he asked, "Did you grow up around here?"

She took the napkin from her plate and placed it on her lap, then leaned toward him and said in a low voice, "I sure did. You know how you can tell? If you look around the room at the people who are staring at us, most of them are related to me in some way."

"Even David?" He wasn't sure why he asked that.

He didn't like the way Chelle smiled at the mention of that hulk of a cowboy's name. "No, there are a few people who aren't family, and he's one of them."

Mason frowned. "You two seem close enough."

Chelle gave him a curious look. "In this town, everyone knows everyone else. He runs the ranch that abuts my parents' place. It'd be strange if I didn't know him."

A sudden thought came to Mason that hadn't occurred to him before. "Are your parents here?"

Chelle nodded toward one corner of the reception hall. "See the man over there glaring at you and the woman who is practically clapping because I'm talking to a man? That's them."

Well, that's one way to kill an erection.

Mason looked at the other guests at the table and realized they were listening to every word he and Chelle said. He leaned closer to her. "I'm not really hungry. Do you want to get some fresh air?"

"Yes. I'd love to." Her eyes met his, and they lit with a hunger that drew an equally strong reaction from him.

Shit. This is probably a bad idea. That fact didn't stop him, however, from standing up and offering his arm to Chelle. She took it, and they made their way to the hall exit.

They walked through the hotel foyer, which led to a balcony overlooking a courtyard garden. He and Chelle continued on to one corner of it. He didn't want anyone to hear what he had to say. "I realize you don't know me, Chelle, but there is something I'm hoping you'll help me with."

"I feel exactly the same way," Chelle said and slid her arms around his neck. Before he had time to respond, she'd pulled his head down and was kissing him.

And that's all it took for Mason to forget all about Trish Shugarts and her threats. He pulled Chelle closer and gave himself over to the hottest kiss of his life. Her lips eagerly parted for his tongue. Her body molded itself to his. It wasn't simply that she wanted him. Many women had given themselves to him with every bit as much enthusiasm. But somehow, this time, it felt less like a new adventure and more like a journey home.

The idea shook him, but not enough to break off the kiss. He claimed her mouth with his, loving how her tongue teased by withdrawing before joining his again. She was both bold and shy at the same time, a combination that had him wild with images of how she'd respond in his bed.

The knowledge that they were in a public place held Mason back from taking their kiss to the next level, but just barely. He moved on to kiss her jaw, the curve of her neck. God, he wanted to rip her dress off right there and take her.

"This is exactly how I always imagined it would be," Chelle said in awe, arching her neck to give him better access.

"What?" he asked absently. He was really much more interested in kissing his way down to her breasts than hearing her answer.

"Sex. I'm so glad I waited."

Her words poured over Mason like a bucket of ice. He froze and raised his head. "How old are you?"

She squirmed against him. "Twenty-five."

"So you're not a . . ."

A cautious expression spread across her face. "Would it matter if I were?"

Virgins had been on his no-touch list for over a decade. With a hand firmly on each of her arms, he held her back from him. "Unfortunately, yes. Sorry, I lost my head for a minute there. This wasn't even why I asked you out here."

She tensed beneath his hands, and her cheeks went bright red. "It's a problem, isn't it? I thought this would happen at twenty-six, but I can see it in your eyes. I waited too long, didn't I?"

Mason was normally a smooth talker, but when he opened his mouth to answer her, he was momentarily stumped. He was as shocked by what she'd said as his own response to it. He should be running for the hills, but he was still holding on to her. "There's nothing wrong with being a virgin."

She rolled her eyes and let out a frustrated huff. "Really? Then why are you looking at me like I have a disease you're afraid of catching?"

He was afraid, but not the way she thought. He liked the idea that no one had ever been with her. He liked it much more than he was comfortable with. Outside of his career, he didn't consider himself a man with much honor, but Chelle deserved better than a one-night stand with someone who was looking for a cover story to save his ass from another woman. "If you've waited this long, Chelle, you should hook up with a nice man from here and . . ."

She pulled her arms free from his grasp and folded them over her chest, an act that had the front of her dress gaping open, giving him a tantalizing view of a black lace bra with—*Is that a condom tucked in the side of it?* Mason swallowed hard.

"There are no men here. That's the problem. None that I've ever felt anything for." She let out an angry breath and turned away. "Forget it. This was a stupid idea. You're probably awful in bed anyway."

Mason surprised himself by blocking her exit from the corner of the balcony. "I'm actually considered gifted in that department."

Chelle rolled her eyes and shook her head. "That's what all men think. Ask any woman and she'll tell you. You can't all be the best."

With his pride smarting, Mason said, "Once women have been with me, they find it difficult to move on. Actually, I brought you out here to ask for your help with that. I slept with a woman I shouldn't have, and to get her to back off I told her I was seeing someone."

Chelle met his eyes with confusion. "And what did you hope I would do?"

"I'd like to take a few pictures of us together. And if anyone asks, I'd like you to say we've been together for a while."

"Why do you think I'd be okay with that?"

"I could pay you. Or, if you'd like a trip to California, I could fly you out there for a while. All expenses paid. No strings attached. No expectations."

Her eyes narrowed. "You mean no sex."

He pocketed his hands and shrugged. Her tone confused him, and he was already regretting bringing up the idea. It had held a lot more appeal before he'd kissed her. Now he didn't know if he could travel with her and keep his hands off her, but that wasn't an admission he was willing to make.

The slap she gave him full across the face took him completely by surprise. Her chest was heaving angrily, beautifully. "That's for making me think you wanted me."

She raised her hand again, but he caught it before she could connect. A primal desire surged through him. He wanted to pull her to him again and kiss her until she was offering herself to him once again. He didn't, though. He didn't think he could stop if they started up again, and the balcony was not private enough to prove to her that she was wrong about why he'd turned her down. "I didn't mean to hurt you."

She pulled her hand free of his. "You didn't. To hurt me, you'd have to be someone I care about. All you did was confirm that I need to get the hell out of Fort Mavis."

With that, she walked away.

Mason stood on the balcony for a long time after she left, rubbing the cheek she'd smacked and telling himself that he'd made the right choice. Sleeping with Chelle would have complicated an already difficult situation.

Chapter Three

Chelle rushed blindly across the hotel lobby. It was one thing to have never been with a man because her standards were too high or she was waiting for love, but to have offered herself to a man only to realize that he had zero interest in her . . . well, that was a real kick to her ego.

She made her way into the bathroom and locked the door behind her. A look in the mirror confirmed that her makeup was smeared from tears she hadn't known were pouring down her face. *Dammit.* She grabbed a tissue and tried to make herself look less like a raccoon.

When she finished, she studied her reflection with a critical eye. *I'm not ugly. I mean, there's no obvious deformity to my face. I'm reasonably fit. I could lose ten pounds, but who couldn't? No, I'm not a model, but those people don't exist outside of magazines, do they? My hair could be blonder. My breasts could definitely be bigger. Do men prefer women who are taller?* She forced a smile onto her face, a smile that became a pained grimace. *What is it that he found unattractive?*

She reached into her bra, pulled out the condom, and stared at it in her hand. *I should have kept my mouth shut about my inexperience. But that's me. I blurt things out when I'm excited.*

The memory of their kiss brought a flush to Chelle's cheeks. She looked up at her reflection and saw desire burning in her eyes. Regardless of how the kiss had made Mason feel, it was obvious how she still felt about it.

Mason Thorne does not matter. What he thinks of me does not affect how I see myself. It's okay to be a twenty-five-year-old virgin. The right man will appreciate that I waited for him.

Fresh tears came to her eyes, and she dabbed them quickly away. *I am so full of shit. I should probably sleep with Bobby Mulner just to get it over with.*

Despite how he had become an attractive adult, she shuddered at the thought of kissing him. *Maybe if I got drunk. Isn't that what everyone does the first time? They have a few too many and blame it on that?*

There is not enough alcohol here to make Bobby look good to me.

Shaking her head, Chelle turned, unlocked the bathroom door, and stepped back into the foyer only to come face-to-face with one very concerned-looking David. *Double shit.*

"What happened, Chelle?"

Her bottom lip quivered, and she shrugged. "I'm an idiot." She looked away. It was then she realized she still had the condom in her hand. She held it out to him. "Here. I won't be needing this."

David accepted it with a carefully blank expression and dropped it into his jacket pocket.

Out of the corner of her eye, Chelle caught a glimpse of her father at the door of the reception hall and hoped age had diminished his eyesight. He didn't look happy as he turned on his heel and disappeared back into the reception.

She fisted her hands at her sides.

David studied her face for a moment more, then, in his always unflappably calm manner, suggested, "Why don't I go get Melanie for you?"

Before Chelle could tell him it wasn't necessary, he also retreated back into the wedding reception. Only the knowledge that things would get worse rather than better if she left made her do the same.

Melanie was at her side a moment later, pulling her off to a quiet area away from the music. "Do you need a pad or tampon? I don't have a purse with me, but one of my sisters will."

Confused, Chelle shook her head. "Why would you ask that?" Then she spun in horror, trying to see the back of her dress. "Oh my God, did I start?" *I didn't think things could get worse, but I was wrong.*

Melanie raised a hand in a calming motion. "No. No. David told me you were having feminine issues and sent me over. I just assumed . . ."

Panic receded as Chelle saw the root of the misunderstanding. She rubbed a hand over her eyes, not sure if she was on the verge of laughing or crying again. "This may very well be the worst day of my life."

Melanie made a face and joked. "I wouldn't let Sarah hear you say that." When Chelle didn't even crack a smile, Melanie added, "How bad could today be? I saw you talking to Mason; I'm sure that was entertaining."

"Trust me—it wasn't."

"Did he say something to upset you?" Melanie closed a hand on Chelle's forearm. "You can tell me."

Unable to meet Melanie's eyes, Chelle said, "I'm not myself tonight. Can we leave it at that? I want to have a drink, maybe two, and start tonight over. I've been a total ass so far, but that ends now. Tonight is about Sarah and Tony, not me." *And my cobwebbed vagina.*

Melanie looked as if she wanted to ask another question, but instead she nodded. "Okay, but if you need to talk to someone, I'm here, Chelle. We may not be as close as you and Sarah, but I don't like to see you upset."

Chelle studied the woman who had spent so many years hiding from the world. She remembered falsely believing Melanie didn't want friends. Melanie used to always have an unapproachable, angry expression on her face, but she had changed over the past year. She was softer, more confident, and a hundred times more beautiful.

She looked over at Charles Dery, Melanie's fiancé, and smiled at him sadly. *I'm happy she found him. And that Sarah found Tony. Just because Mason Thorne didn't want me doesn't mean the right man isn't right around the corner.*

Who knows, maybe he'll walk right through that door.

The side door of the reception hall opened, and Chelle held her breath. Fate had never been overly kind to her, but after the day she'd had, maybe it felt it owed her.

A woman walked in, decked out in a skintight silver dress and diamonds. Her hair was done up in a beautiful loose knot, and she carried herself like a princess arriving at a ball. "Who is that?" Chelle asked aloud.

Melanie turned and also gave the newcomer a once-over. "I have no idea, but she appears to be looking for someone."

Flashy to the point of being gaudy. Beautiful in a plastic sort of way. The woman belonged in Hollywood, not some tiny town in Texas. *Hollywood.*

Could she be the woman Mason claimed he had lied to in an attempt to discourage her? Could she? If so, Chelle found it difficult to feel sympathy for her. The Gwyneth Paltrow blonde made a face as she looked around the room, as if she had entered an unclean area she couldn't wait to leave. She wrinkled her nose at one of Chelle's slightly overweight female cousins, who had squeezed herself into a dress that had probably fit her well at the last wedding she'd attended.

A protective shot of adrenaline coursed through Chelle. *Oh no you don't. I don't care what they're wearing—you do not look at my family like that.* Chelle almost headed straight over to confront her, but stopped when a better option occurred to her.

She wasn't sure if her motivation stemmed from feeling protective of her family or from not liking the idea of Mason with someone so obviously superficial. Either way, Mason had asked for help, whatever his reaction to her. Sending Barbie scurrying back to California felt like the right thing to do.

"Are you okay, Chelle?" Melanie asked when Chelle turned to walk away without saying anything.

"I will be."

Mason rested his elbows on the banister of the balcony, trying to untangle his thoughts before returning to the wedding. He'd decided a long time ago that guilt was a wasted emotion. It didn't change anything.

Still, he didn't like how he felt each time he thought about Chelle. He'd been honest with her. Wasn't that better than leading her on?

I could have let her down easier. She doesn't know how badly I wanted to say yes to her.

David appeared beside him and mirrored his pensive pose. "I remember my first impression of you."

Mason straightened, turned to lean back against the railing, and folded his arms across his chest. David sounded like a man about to give a stern lecture to a child, and frankly, Mason wasn't in the mood. "I'm sure I don't want to hear it."

Without missing a beat, David continued, "I thought you were a self-serving, irreverent narcissist."

Mason raised an eyebrow, refusing to rise to the very obvious bait. "My, my," he said with thick sarcasm and a fake southern accent, "that must be what they call southern charm."

"Consider it a dose of Texan honesty."

Mason turned to meet David's eyes. "Let me give you some Californian candor. I couldn't care less what you think of me."

David straightened, but kept both hands tight on the railing. "A wedding is no place for disagreements, but I wouldn't feel right if I didn't speak my mind. You need to stay away from Chelle Landon."

Mason barked out a laugh. "You're upset because you saw me talking to a woman?"

David's hands clenched visibly. "Chelle is one of the sweetest, shyest women in these parts."

Mason's eyes rounded a bit in disbelief. During his very brief acquaintance with her, Chelle had both kissed him and belted him. David, however, didn't look like a man who would appreciate Mason's insights into her character. "I'm sure she is."

"Someone like you would be better off steering clear of her."

"Someone like me?" Some of Mason's appreciation for the humor of the situation faded. "I'm a goddamned senator."

"What you do for a living has no bearing on what I'm saying. I'm telling you to find your entertainment elsewhere tonight."

Mason pushed off the banister and turned to face David. "Listen, David, I like you. I do. In fact, this whole small-town good-guy persona you have going is big-screen worthy. However, Chelle doesn't need your protection, and I'm in no mood to humor you. This conversation is over."

David's eyes narrowed in anger. He straightened to his full height, which was about equal to Mason's. "My 'good-guy persona' will shove its boot up your ass if I see you around Chelle again tonight."

Mason flashed his teeth at David and leaned in threateningly. "I didn't get where I am today by letting anyone tell me what I could and couldn't do. I don't want to fight with you, David. Not at a wedding, but if you take it there, you won't like the outcome."

"You think you'd last longer than a second in a real fight?" David went nose to nose with him. "Your confidence is overblown from those fancy gym punching bags. Don't make me prove it to you."

"So this is where the party is," Charles said, deliberately making light of the tension between the two men. "They're cutting the cake inside, but it might be best if you two stay out here until they put the knife away."

Neither Mason nor David looked away from their standoff.

Charles admonished them. "Seriously, whatever you're arguing about, shelve it for tonight. This is a big day for my sister. I want people to remember her wedding because it was beautiful, not because you two jackasses had a drunken brawl."

"One drink," Mason said tightly.

"Stone sober," David added.

"Then what the fuck is the problem?" Charles asked impatiently.

"No problem. I believe I made my point." David gave Mason one last warning look before walking away.

Mason held back the smart-ass retort that came to him, but only out of respect for what Charles had just said. It was, after all, his best friend's sister's wedding. "You must love it here, Charlie. These people are as uptight as you are."

"What point did he feel he needed to make?" Charles asked.

Mason shrugged. "He saw me talking to Chelle and couldn't handle it."

Charles rocked back on his heels and pocketed his hands in his trousers. "Stay away from her, Mace. She's not like the women you're used to."

Mason rubbed the cheek she'd slapped. "So I'm beginning to see."

"I'm serious. Most of these people were born here. They marry local, and they intend to die here. Some families settled here generations ago. Reputations matter. Don't do anything that will make it hard for Chelle to face her neighbors tomorrow."

"You mean, don't do anything that will make it hard for *you*."

"That too."

Mason let out a long sigh. "Do you want me to leave? You know, before I corrupt the whole town?"

Charles ran a hand through his hair. "No. You're a good friend, and it means a lot to Sarah that you came. You were late, but you came."

"Maybe I would have gotten here quicker if your sister hadn't decided to marry someone in cow-tipping country."

Charles gave a flicker of a smile at that. "It's not that bad." Then he sobered. "You really don't have any business messing with someone like Chelle. She's a good woman. She deserves . . ."

Mason frowned. "Someone better?"

Charles pinched the bridge of his nose and seemed to be choosing his words carefully. "You're with a different woman every night. Sometimes more than one at a time. I don't judge your lifestyle—"

Irritation spread through Mason. "It sure as hell sounds like you do."

"Mason, I get why you don't let yourself get attached to women. What you do with your personal life isn't my business, unless you bring it here. I don't know how to say this any more nicely. I'm happy with Melanie. The next wedding this town sees will likely be ours. If you fuck that up for me, I don't know if we could get past it."

"How much of a bastard do you think I am?"

Charles didn't say a word, but his silence was his answer.

"That's just fucking great," Mason said harshly. He shook his head in disgust. "Believe it or not, I have no intention of having sex with anyone in this godforsaken town. Saint Chelle is safe. I'll fly out right after the reception."

"Thank you," Charles said, then smiled. "How about we go get some cake?"

Slightly offended by how his friend had readily agreed that he should go, Mason gave Charles a long, dark look.

Chelle walked back onto the balcony. She smiled at Charles. "Do you mind if I speak to Mason alone?"

Despite how his heart started pounding at Chelle's entrance, Mason gave Charles a pointed look, then said to Chelle, "Charles was just explaining that my presence is requested back inside."

Chelle laid a hand on Mason's arm. The heat of that innocent touch shot through him, making it difficult to concentrate on her next words. "It'll just take a minute. There's something you need to know."

Mason's imagination was running overtime. Was she back to offer herself to him again? If so, he didn't think he could say no, regardless of what he'd promised Charles. With an inward groan, Mason said, "I shouldn't."

Charles made a warning sound deep in his throat.

Mason strengthened his refusal. "I won't." He looked at Chelle and silently implored her to understand. "I appreciate whatever you came to say, but I really have to go inside."

"Mason, darling, there you are," a high-pitched female voice sang loudly from a few feet away.

"Trish," Mason said between gritted teeth. *Fuck. This isn't going to be pretty.* He was still weighing his exit options in his head when, to his utter shock, Chelle tucked herself beneath one of his arms.

"Mason? Is this one of your California friends?"

"Oh, honey, I'm more than his friend."

Chelle gasped and brought a shaking hand to her mouth. The frantic look she gave him was Emmy worthy. "Tell me this isn't the woman you cheated on me with." She let out a tiny sob.

The actor in Mason admired the emotion Chelle was bringing to the scene. He didn't understand why she'd changed her mind about helping him, and if Charles's expression was anything to go by, there would be hell to pay for this later, but for the moment playing along with her made sense. "It is, but it's over, Chelle. I meant everything I said. She was a mistake, and one I'm sorry for."

Trish's eyes narrowed, and she wrinkled her nose. "Mason, you can't be seriously dating this . . . this . . ."

Chelle leaned forward in mock sympathy for the other woman. "Don't hold back on my account. I understand why you're upset. You came all this way to see a man who is in love with someone else. So let it out if you have to. We've all been there."

Trish's face went bright red beneath her thick makeup. "You bitch."

Mason straightened in anger. "I think it would be best if you left, Trish."

The blonde scoffed. "You're threatening me?"

Mason pulled Chelle closer to his side and returned to the improv Chelle had initiated. "No, I'm asking you to respect that I've found a woman I care deeply for." He looked down at Chelle. "I know I have to win back her trust, but she is worth every hoop she has me jump through to make that happen."

"Oh please," Trish said with disgust. "You would choose her over me?"

Without looking away from Chelle's eyes, Mason said, "Every day for the rest of my life."

Chelle raised a hand and gazed lovingly up into Mason's eyes. "I've changed my mind. I accept your proposal, Mason Thorne. I do want to settle down with you and have those six children you keep talking about."

"Six children?" Trish repeated in disgust. "You can have him. No man is worth those stretch marks." Trish snorted and flounced off.

Mason was momentarily mesmerized by Chelle and the feelings her words had elicited in him. He knew it was all an act, and he'd always been able to keep that straight during his acting career, but this felt different. Words that should have terrified the confirmed bachelor in him lit a yearning in him he'd never felt before.

He'd never met a woman he could imagine waking up to more than once. In fact, he preferred their time together end well before that. Love was a mystery he was not at all interested in unraveling. He'd watched his friends pair off and always wondered why they would possibly choose one woman when they could have many.

Still, he couldn't deny how he'd felt when Chelle had said she would marry him. For just one insane moment, he'd felt as if he weren't alone. Until then, he hadn't considered that he might not want to be.

Chelle pushed back from him. "You really are a dog," she said in a scathing tone and walked away.

Mason simply stood there watching her go, wondering how one woman could have knocked him so off kilter.

Charles cleared his throat loudly again. "I don't want to know what any of that was about. Just promise me you'll keep it out of the damn wedding reception." With that, he also left.

Mason returned to his pensive stance, looking out into the night. Trish Shugarts was very likely upset enough with him to say something nasty about him to her father. Suddenly, that possibility didn't matter. He'd weather that storm as he'd weathered all the others in his career.

No, the only problem in his life was a five-foot-two natural blonde.

And the raging hard-on she'd left him with.

Chapter Four

Chelle walked into the reception with her head held high. She couldn't deny it had felt good to stand up to that woman. She wasn't the least bit sorry about putting her in her place. *Thought you could come here and look down your nose at us? Think again, sweetheart. There's a reason people say you don't mess with Texas. Even the sweetest of us can dole out an ass-whupping when we come across a person in need of one.*

She also didn't regret telling Mason what she thought of him. Sure, he was gorgeous, but he had an ego the size of the state he represented. Chelle rolled her eyes skyward and reviewed her behavior over the past few hours. *I can't even imagine what Mason thinks of me. I chase him around like a horny teenager, I smack him, then pretty much propose to him. If I keep this up, I'm going to end up on some government watch list.*

Melanie spotted her and walked over with Charles. She looked Chelle over, then gave Charles a look. "Chelle, is everything okay? You sprinted out of here in such a hurry I thought you were upset."

Chelle looked into Charles's carefully expressionless face, then back at Melanie. "Weddings are emotional, even when they aren't your own. I lost my head for a minute there, but I'm fine now."

Melanie turned to her fiancé. "Charles, could you get me a soda water and lemon? Chelle, would you like something?"

"No, thank you."

After Charles gave Melanie a quick kiss on the cheek and walked away, Melanie said softly, "Your turn will come, Chelle."

Knowing the trials Melanie had gone through and how her life had turned around gave Chelle hope in that moment. "I know it will. I just don't know if I can find what I want in this town, Mel."

"I guess that depends on what you're yearning for."

Chelle looked across the reception hall at her parents. "I'm twenty-five. Do you know how many times I've been out of Texas? Zero. I love my parents, but living on their ranch and helping them run it is all I know. Did you ever look at yourself in the mirror and think, I thought I'd be more than this?"

"Yes, I did," Melanie said quietly. "I remember that feeling too well."

"But you did something about it."

Melanie started to shake her head, then stopped herself. "I was about to say Charles did, but you're right: it was me. I finished my degree, and even though I'm engaged, I'm still running my interior design business. My mother always said people should never be a destination, but rather a partner for the road. I like to think that's what I am with Charles. Before I could invite him to be part of my journey, though, I had to find out for myself what my journey was. It sounds like that's where you are. Where would you go if you could go anywhere? What would you do if you thought anything was possible?"

Possibilities were sometimes as terrifying as they were exciting to consider. "I used to want to travel. I was accepted to Boston College. I didn't know what I wanted to do, but I felt I could make a difference. Then my grandmother passed away, and there was no one to watch my grandfather during the day. If I'd had sisters or brothers, maybe I could have gone away to a state school, but instead I took classes online so I could get my degree and live at home while everyone else worked."

Melanie said softly, "It sounds like you did make a difference."

Chelle nodded. "I don't regret any of the decisions I've made. I was holding my grandfather's hand when he passed away. I have a degree in accounting, and I've been able to help my parents weather some financial storms. I'm sorry. I don't mean to bring up sad topics—it's just that I started thinking today about all the things I haven't done yet, and I panicked." She looked across the room and caught Mason watching her. Her cheeks warmed when she remembered how she'd thrown herself at him, only to have him explain that sex hadn't been what he'd wanted from her. Perhaps he had done her a favor. If he had said yes, he would have been her destination, albeit probably only for that one night. Instead, he'd brought her full circle, back to a place where she needed to once again ask herself what she really wanted. Was it really a one-night stand? Would she regret it? She'd waited so long for someone to look at her the way Tony had gazed down at Sarah when he'd said his vows. Did not wanting to wait anymore mean she was settling? Giving up?

I'm going to die a virgin.

"Chelle, I know you well enough to know you're sitting on enough money to go somewhere if you want to. So maybe you should. Life is too short to live it feeling as if you've missed out. Pick a destination and go. Your parents are fine. And who knows, you might discover everything you want is back here. Or discover something you love out there."

"I can't go by myself."

Melanie gave her a pointed look. "Because you're scared?"

"Shitless," Chelle added with humor. "This is all I know."

Melanie shrugged. "I completely understand that, too. I let my fears hold me back for a long time. I don't have all the answers, Chelle, but I do know one thing. You can't see the world if you never leave Texas."

Mason folded his arms across his chest and leaned against a wall near the side exit. He considered leaving the reception early, but he couldn't. As Chelle moved from one table to another, his fascination with her grew. Both David and Charles had described Chelle as a sweet woman, someone they didn't want him to lead astray. How was she also the brazen beauty who had kissed him with a condom tucked in her bra? As he watched her interact with her friends and family, he saw a woman who had an extra-warm smile for both children and the elderly. A woman who seemed to know and like everyone. There had to be someone she had issues with. Someone she'd reveal she had no patience for.

No one is that fucking perfect.

He told himself curiosity was the only reason he couldn't look away. He didn't want to acknowledge that there was more. She was alluring in ways that were difficult for him to align with his usual partners. By his jaded standards, Trish should have been more appealing to him. Like many of the women he knew, Trish obviously prioritized her physical appearance. Endless hours in the gym. Salads with a portion of protein but no dressing. Every imperfection in her features had been professionally smoothed away.

He watched Chelle adjust her bodice again as she walked from one table to another, and smiled. He would bet she couldn't wait to get home and take off that dress.

The idea brought his cock instantly back to attention, an uncomfortable state of affairs considering the table she'd joined. He recognized the man and woman as her parents. She was standing beside her father when she turned and sought Mason's eyes.

My God, you're beautiful. I can't believe you've never been with anyone. The things I could teach you about yourself. Something tells me you'd be worth whatever trouble being with you brought.

Her father said something, and Chelle blushed, then turned away again. A moment later, her laughter rang out, and he wondered if the comment had been about him. Her father sent him a brief glare, and Mason fought back a guilty smile.

He knows what I'm thinking.

Chelle glanced at him again with a shy smile. *She, however, has no idea.* She leaned down and made one last comment to her parents, then began walking in his direction.

His breath caught in his throat and his heart beat crazily in his chest. Behind her, he saw Charles give a curt shake of his head.

I know. I know.

Mason pushed off the wall and exited the reception hall. He was halfway across the foyer and headed toward the stairs when he heard her voice.

"Mason, there's something I need to say before you go."

Mason groaned and stopped without turning around. *I am only human.* "I have to meet my plane. I'm flying out tonight."

She stepped in front of him and looked up. The siren of earlier had been replaced by an earnest innocent. "I want to apologize for my behavior tonight. I don't know what came over me. I've never hit anyone in my life." She chewed her bottom lip. "And I shouldn't have called you a dog. I don't know anything about you, and I only said it because my pride was smarting."

He stood there staring at her, digesting what she'd said. He'd expected her to try to give him one final cutting remark. Or to make another play for him. He didn't quite know what her agenda was. Women always had one. "No need to apologize. You made up for hitting me by convincing Trish we were together."

She smiled wryly. "I'm glad it worked out the way you wanted it to."

He frowned at her instead of answering. Glad wasn't how he would describe how he felt. Part of him wanted to push her, see if a little temper would bring back the passionate woman he'd glimpsed within her. *Leave well enough alone,* he warned himself.

She held out a hand for him to shake. "Since you're close with Charles, I'm sure this won't be the last time we see each other. If you can forget my temporary lapse in sanity tonight, maybe we can be friends."

Mason wrapped his hand around hers and simply held it. Her grip was strong and honest. Her lips, the ones that had sought his earlier, pursed sweetly as if she were holding back something she wanted to say. "Friends?"

She pulled her hand back and hugged it to her, seeming suddenly less sure. "Why not? I'll admit I was embarrassed earlier, but my grandfather always said people are only as happy as they make up their minds to be. So I'm looking for the positive in us meeting. I'm grateful it worked out as it did."

The more she spoke, the less happy he was. "That you didn't leave with me?"

She smiled with shyness, and it took everything in him not to pull her into his arms. "Yes. I do want the first time to be with someone I care about. I appreciate how you respected that. Awkward as this conversation is, I wanted to say thank you."

"Glad I could help," Mason said tightly and turned on his heel. He needed to get out of Texas and away from the woman who had succeeded in tying his insides up into a hundred painful knots.

Chapter Five

Two weeks later, Chelle was sitting with Sarah and Melanie in Sarah's living room. It was the second time that week she'd been invited over for lunch. The discussion the last time had been mostly about the Hawaiian honeymoon Sarah and Tony had just returned from and the little they had actually seen outside their presidential suite. Both Melanie and Sarah looked like they were bursting to tell her something.

Could one of them be pregnant?

Did Melanie and Charles pick a date?

Chelle had done some serious reflecting since her freak-out at Sarah's wedding. She refused to be the kind of person who couldn't be happy for her friends just because they were in a better place than she was. In that spirit, she smiled and asked, "I can't take it anymore. Spill whatever it is you two are sitting on."

Sarah clasped her hands on her lap. "I spoke to Josie. She said you had gone to her travel agency and picked up some brochures last week, but she hadn't heard from you since."

Chelle's smile faltered. That wasn't at all what she'd expected her to say. "I've been busy."

Melanie leaned forward, and her skepticism was obvious. "Is that all it is?"

Chelle looked away and shrugged, not comfortable with sharing what she didn't want to admit even to herself. "Sure. You were right. I do want to travel. I just haven't had time to decide where I want to go."

Sarah reached behind a cushion on her couch and pulled out a small gift-wrapped box. "I was hoping you'd say that." She held the box out to Chelle. "I made this for you, but before you open it, I want you to promise me something."

Chelle took the gift and held it on her lap while watching her two friends cautiously. "I've never gotten a gift that came with conditions before."

Sarah's smile widened. "Then today is your lucky day."

Melanie nodded toward the box. "Sarah made it, but I have to admit I like the idea."

Chelle lifted the gift and shook it. The contents sounded like pieces of cardboard sliding back and forth. As her curiosity grew, she started to unwrap it, but Sarah quickly placed her hand on it to stop her.

"First, you have to promise to use it."

Looking back and forth between Sarah and Melanie, Chelle said, "How can I do that before I know what it is?"

Melanie shared a look with Sarah.

Sarah waved a hand at the still-unopened gift. "Do you trust us?"

Chelle thought about how good both of them had been to her. Sarah had been open and kind since the first day she'd met her. And Melanie, well, she took longer to open up, but underneath her tough exterior, she was actually pretty sweet. Neither had ever given her a reason to doubt their friendship. "Absolutely."

Sarah pointed to the box again. "Then just promise. Let us help you change your life."

Melanie raised and dropped one shoulder. "I wouldn't have said it so dramatically, but I do think it's a nice idea."

Chelle tipped the box again, trying to guess the contents from the sound inside. What could she possibly use that would come with life-changing rules? "You're serious?"

Sarah nodded forcefully. "Swear to follow the rules before you open it." When Chelle didn't agree immediately, Sarah held out her hand. "Of course, if you're too afraid to do that, you can always give it back to me."

Chelle tightened her hands on the gift. Her fears were already holding her back from leaving town; she wouldn't let them stop her from opening a silly little present. "I swear."

Sarah clapped her hands. "Then open it."

Chelle ripped the white wrapping paper off, revealing a simple cardboard box. She removed the tape that held it closed and reached inside. Her hand closed around what felt like a deck of cards. She pulled one out and studied it. It was a regular shiny playing card with a photo of Niagara Falls taped to one side of it. She looked at Sarah in confusion.

Sarah said softly, "Josie gave us a list of everywhere you had taken information about. I glued each destination on a different card and put all of them in there. Now all you have to do is close your eyes, stick your hand in there, and let fate decide where you should go."

Chelle pulled out a handful of the cards and fanned them out. It was just as Sarah had said. From Paris to Alaska, each represented one of the many places she'd always dreamed of visiting. She dropped the cards back in the box and looked at Sarah and Melanie through tear-filled eyes. "I can't believe you did this for me."

Sarah's eyes shone with emotion. "We both know what it's like to feel trapped. I can't speak for Melanie, but I was my own roadblock. It took coming to Texas to break me free. Now I feel like I could go anywhere—do anything. I just happen to want to be here."

Melanie gave Sarah a hug. "For me, it took watching you charge forward with your life to get me to believe there was something I could do about my own."

"And now you and Jace spend your holidays traveling with Charles. Did you ever think you'd be a world traveler?"

Melanie met Chelle's eyes. "Never. I didn't think I deserved more than I had, and I was afraid to open myself up to disappointment again. Maybe we're wrong, Chelle, but is that where you are?"

Chelle wiped away a stray tear. She hugged the box to her stomach and nodded.

"Then decide today that you are going to take a leap of faith," Sarah said cheerfully. "Pick a card and go wherever the card tells you to. No second-guessing. No procrastinating. Take that card to Josie today and choose your first adventure."

"I'm doing it. Here goes." Hope replaced fear. Chelle put her hand into the cardboard box and closed her eyes. She shuffled through the cards, fervently hoping the right choice would come to her. In a comically dramatic voice, Chelle said, "Oh, magical recycled cardboard box, help me choose where I should go. Show me my destiny."

She pulled out a card and held her breath. Would she be buying a bikini, hiking boots, or tickets to a Broadway show? Wherever the card said, she suddenly felt ready to embrace it. Her heart was beating wildly when she finally opened her eyes.

Disappointment quickly followed as she looked at what she had chosen. "The paper must have fallen off this one. It's just the king of hearts." An image of Mason came to her, but she dismissed it as ridiculous. She tossed the card on the table. "I appreciate what you're trying to do with this game, Sarah, but maybe this isn't how I should make a big decision like this."

Sarah picked up the card from the table. "Wait. How do you know this isn't it?"

Chelle put the box aside, brought her legs up onto the edge of the couch, and hugged her knees to her chest. "A blank card? If that's really an answer, then what does it mean? That I'm not meant to go anywhere?"

Sarah turned the card around between her fingers. "Or you're not supposed to go alone. The king of hearts. Maybe the love of your life is waiting for you at the destination you choose."

Melanie rolled her eyes. "Or, Sarah, you didn't use strong enough glue."

Sarah swatted at Melanie. "Don't discourage her. You agreed this was a good idea."

With a sigh, Melanie conceded the point. "Fine. Please pull another card, Chelle, or I'll never hear the end of this."

Chelle glanced at the box with doubt. She didn't really want to raise her hopes again, but in the face of her friends' urging, she didn't see a whole lot of options. She reached inside again, this time not bothering to even close her eyes, and pulled out the first card her fingers brushed.

Sarah grabbed the card as Chelle tossed it on the table, and exclaimed, "The Golden Gate Bridge. You're going to California!" She turned to Melanie. "Mason is out there. I bet he has single friends he could introduce her to. Oh my God, that's perfect."

The heat of a blush spread up Chelle's neck and warmed her cheeks. "I should pick again."

"Oh no," Sarah said as if she were a high authority. "You have your answer. Besides, you told me you were concerned about traveling alone. Now you don't have to. You'll have someone who can show you around. Trust me, Mason won't mind. I've known him half my life. He talks like he thinks he's God's gift to women, but he's a good guy. Just tell him you're not into the wild crowd."

"I can't," Chelle said curtly.

Melanie shot a pained smile at Sarah. "You were too busy to notice, Sarah, but Chelle and Mason had a little thing at your wedding."

"A thing?" Sarah asked.

Chelle tucked a long blonde curl behind one of her ears. "It was nothing."

"Oh, it was something," Melanie countered. "Charles wasn't really happy with him about it, but they've both gotten over it."

Sarah waved both hands in the air. "Hold on. Rewind. What did I miss?"

Chelle grimaced and admitted, "I may have kissed Mason at the reception."

"Oh." Sarah bit her lip. "Chelle, he's a huge flirt. He probably kissed ten women that night."

"I was the only single woman there," Chelle said in protest.

Sarah bobbed her head a few times. "That doesn't always matter to Mason." She studied Chelle's face intently for a moment. "Do you have any feelings for him?"

"No," Chelle said slowly.

"Then California is still an option. Trust me, to Mason a kiss is like a handshake. He'll be perfectly fine introducing you to his friends."

This is awkward. "I can't meet his friends."

"Why not?" With a sigh, Sarah admonished her. "You have to stop thinking in terms of what you can't do, and just grab this idea by the balls." When her choice of words elicited a laugh from both Melanie and Chelle, Sarah waved her hand dismissively in the air. "You know what I mean."

"I do," Chelle said with a smile. "But there is a reason why Mason probably won't want to introduce me to anyone he knows out there." Melanie's eyebrows rose, and Sarah motioned for her to continue. "I'm his fake fiancée." She gave in and recounted how she had thought Mason liked her, but had learned he'd really wanted to hire her to discourage some fling he'd been having trouble ending. She left out the part about asking David for a condom and kept her focus on how she and Mason had pretended they were a serious couple.

Sarah glared playfully at Melanie. "I can't believe you didn't tell me any of this."

Melanie shrugged. "I didn't know."

"So you're fake engaged to Mason Thorne?" Sarah asked with wonder.

Chelle made a pained face. "I guess? Unless we fake broke up? I haven't spoken to him since."

Sarah hopped to her feet. "You have to call him."

Chelle vehemently shook her head.

That didn't deter Sarah in the least. "Oh, come on. Where's your sense of adventure? I would head right out there and play along that I was engaged to him. Imagine the parties you could attend. Have some fun."

Chelle stood, too, and wrapped her arms around her waist. "No. It was a mistake to take the game that far in the first place."

Sarah raised a finger in the air and stated, "There are no mistakes in life, just different paths leading to where we are destined to be."

Melanie stood and placed the two cards back in the box. "You say that, Sarah, because you accidentally showered in this house, and that led to you being with Tony."

"Exactly," Sarah said. "I'm happier here than I've ever been anywhere else. All because I made a mistake. And you, Mel, should agree with me. Sure, you talk about how you regret spending years hiding on this ranch with your son, but look how that turned out. Jace is amazing, and you're marrying into my family. You needed to be here, and I needed to get lost or we never would have met. And if you had never met me, you wouldn't have thrown a glass of lemonade in my brother's face and won his heart. See? Fate."

Melanie rubbed her face and laughed. "I can't even argue with her, Chelle. She talks so fast, who can keep up?"

Chelle let herself imagine what Mason would say if she showed up on his doorstep with the intention of perpetuating their cover story. That talk would probably be a lot like the one where he explained that he didn't want to sleep with her. *Yeah, I'll spare myself that.* Chelle glanced at the clock on the wall. "I have a few calls I need to make for my dad, so I should get going. Sarah, I really appreciate the time you put into this. I really do."

"That's it," Sarah exclaimed as inspiration hit her. "We don't have to sit around and wonder if you can go out there or not. We can call Mason and ask him." When Chelle didn't immediately reach for her phone, Sarah asked, "Am I the only one who is dying to know if you two are still engaged?"

Melanie brought a hand to her mouth and said, "Okay, I'm curious."

Chelle took out her cell phone. "First, I don't have his number. Second, what would I say?"

Sarah snatched her phone, typed in a number before hitting "Call," and handed it back to her. "Ask him if his fiancée can come for a visit."

The phone rang once. Twice. Mason's deep voice answered. "Mason Thorne."

Sarah made a grabbing motion with both of her hands. *By the balls.*

Chelle laughed nervously, then cleared her throat. "Hi, Mason, it's me, Chelle Landon."

"Chelle." The way he said her name was a warm caress of its own. "I didn't expect to hear from you."

Chelle took a step back from the two women who were leaning in to hear him. "Is this a bad time? I can call back later if it is."

"No, it's fine. How are you?"

"Good. And you?"

"Why do I have the feeling you didn't call just to see how my day is going?"

"I'm considering a trip to California. I was talking to Sarah about it, and she suggested I contact you. I completely understand if you're too busy, but Sarah said you might enjoy showing me around."

"Enjoy showing you around?" He repeated her request slowly, and Chelle began to doubt herself.

She didn't want him to think she was throwing herself at him again, so she blurted, "She said you could take me to parties and introduce me to your friends. Who knows, I may even hit it off with one of them. That is, unless we're still fake together. Are we? Still together? Because I can go somewhere else if we are."

Mason was quiet for a long moment. "You're calling to ask me to hook you up with one of my friends?"

Chelle closed her eyes in mortification. It really didn't sound good the way he said it. "Not hook up. I don't hook up. I've never . . ." *He knows that. Stop.* Chelle took a deep breath. "I'm sorry. I shouldn't have called."

"Actually," he said slowly, "I'm glad you did. I have a charity dinner coming up this Friday and having you here with me would give my opposition something else to talk about besides their issues with my latest environmental bill. Who knows, you might soothe some ruffled feathers and help me push it through."

"This weekend? As in two days from now?"

"Is that a problem?"

Chelle covered the mouthpiece of her phone and whispered, "We're still engaged. He wants me to attend a dinner with him this weekend."

Sarah hopped with joy. "You have to."

Melanie waved at the phone. "Ask him for the name of a good hotel. Be clear that you're not going out there to be with him." She narrowed her eyes for emphasis. "You're not, are you?"

"Of course not," Chelle said with forced conviction. She removed her hand and said, "Mason, if I'm flying out that soon, I'll need to find a place to stay. Is there a hotel you recommend?"

"I have an extra bedroom in my apartment. You could stay here."

"He said I could stay with him," Chelle echoed.

"No," Melanie said. "If you do that, you'll end up sleeping with him. That's not a good idea. Unless it's what you want."

Sarah waved a hand frantically between them and pointed to the phone. She mouthed, "He can hear you."

Chelle covered her eyes with one hand and put the phone back to her ear. "I'd be more comfortable in a hotel. But I appreciate the offer."

"That's entirely up to you. Text me your flight information, and I'll have everything set up for you on this end."

Mason's tone was so calm that Chelle relaxed. He hadn't heard them. *Thank God.* "I'll do that. Thanks, Mason."

Mason added, "Oh, and tell Melanie I'm flattered she thinks I'm irresistible."

Chelle blushed. "I will," she said with knee-jerk politeness, then hung up on him. She stood there looking down at her phone. "Are we sure this is a good idea? Maybe I should call him back and tell him I changed my mind."

In a matter-of-fact voice, Melanie said, "I guess it all depends which you'd regret more—going or not going."

Sarah gave Chelle a quick hug. "I drove to Texas all by myself. Everyone thought I was insane to do it. It was the best thing I ever did. What's the worst thing that could happen? You go out there and discover you don't like California, Mason, or any of his friends. So what? You come back and pick another destination. Unless you decide that Fort Mavis is where you belong. See, it doesn't matter what I think or what Melanie thinks. What matters is that you let yourself—"

"Grab life by the balls?" Chelle asked with an enthusiastic laugh.

Sarah nodded in approval.

Melanie shook her head, but she was smiling. "I was worried about you, Chelle, but something tells me Mason is the one who'd better be careful."

"I've got to go, darling," Mason said to the ebony beauty lying across the king-size hotel bed. Her cheeks were still flushed from their midmorning lovemaking, her black dreads fanned across his pillow.

Renita sat up and stretched, completely uninhibited. "Me too. My flight leaves in two hours. I was planning to finish my report this morning, but I'm glad I called you. You always send me back to Seattle glowing. Better than a morning at the spa." She picked a white robe off the chair near her bed and slipped it on. "You look happier than usual today. Who was that on the phone?"

Mason had known Renita long enough to not have to hide the truth from her. Plus, he wanted to say it out loud. "My fiancée. She's flying in for the weekend."

Renita laughed. "You are hilarious. As if . . ."

Mason frowned. "I'm not joking."

After giving him a contemplative once-over, Renita laughed again. "You almost had me feeling sorry for some woman. Mason, you are a reliably good fuck, but a woman would have to be insane to marry you." When Mason didn't say anything, Renita walked toward him and met his eyes. She was still chuckling when she said, "Oh my God, you're serious. You're really engaged?"

Mason picked his clothing off the floor and began to get dressed to distract himself from his unexpected anger. "I'm glad you find it so fucking amusing."

"Mason, what did you expect? I mean, if you're so in love, what are you doing still sleeping with other women?"

Mason pulled on his pants with a jerk. Maybe he was excited about the idea of seeing Chelle again, but that was it.

"Mason, I've known you for four years. I lost count of how many times we've hooked up, but I do know it took you about six months before you stopped calling me the wrong name. Honestly, I didn't even care. You're that good. But men like you don't get married."

Mason had never had an issue finding female companionship, but he'd also never asked them what they thought of him. Renita's opinion reminded him why. He pulled on his dress shirt. "As entertaining as this conversation is, I have to get back to my office."

Renita watched him finish dressing, then dug a card out of her purse and held it out to him. "If you really are engaged, you might want to talk to someone about it. This is my therapist's number. She knows all about you and how I use these visits to cheer myself up between boyfriends." As something occurred to her, Renita withdrew the card. "On second thought, she might know too much and want to test-drive you herself."

Shaking his head in disgust, Mason tied the laces on his shoes. He wasn't upset with Renita as much as he was annoyed with himself for caring what she thought of him. "Good-bye, Renita."

Renita stepped between him and the door and searched his face. "What's her name?"

"Chelle Landon."

"What makes you think she's the one?"

Mason was about to deny that Chelle was, but he remembered the first time they'd met. Every moment with her remained as vivid as if only a day had gone by, instead of weeks. "I smile every time I think about her."

"And the sex?" Renita wasn't asking out of jealousy. She and Mason had a friends-with-benefits arrangement, and he could tell she genuinely cared.

"I haven't slept with her yet."

"Engaged to someone you haven't been with? Mason, this is big. Huge. And more than a little fucked up—in a sweet way." She laid a hand on Mason's cheek and gave him a kiss on his other. "I won't call you next time I'm in town. If it doesn't work out with her, call me. But do yourself a favor, and don't sleep with anyone else while you're engaged. Give your relationship a chance."

Mason took Renita's hand in his and gave it a gentle squeeze before letting it drop. "You're a class act, Renita."

As Mason let himself out, he heard her say, "Good luck, Mason."

Mason took the long route back to his office. He needed time to think before he dove back into the meetings booked solid for the rest of the day.

Since he hadn't heard from Trish once in the past two weeks, having Chelle out for a visit was not the wisest choice he'd ever made. No one knew about his fake fiancée. It would be a whole lot simpler to leave it that way.

I should call Chelle back and tell her not to come.

I don't know why I agreed to it in the first place.

He took a corner sharply. If he was honest with himself, her comment about wanting him to introduce her to his friends had put his nose out of joint. He and Chelle made about as much sense as a tiger dating a rabbit, but that hadn't stopped him from fantasizing about her every night. He'd tried to wipe her out of his head by sleeping with other women, but as soon as he'd heard her voice, he'd realized how ineffective that had been.

I might have to sleep with her to get her out of my system.

God, I wish she weren't a virgin.

He ground the gears of his car. Chelle was a dangerous temptation. He already didn't like how she was twisting him on the inside. He felt guilty about sleeping with Renita. Which was ridiculous since he and Chelle hadn't gone on a single date. Until she'd called, he'd had no expectation of hearing from her again. She was under no illusion that either of them had feelings for the other.

Why the fuck did I perpetuate this fake engagement?

Because I don't want her to use that condom she keeps tucked in her bra with someone else.

Shit.

Mason hadn't reached a better mood when he entered his office a little while later. His secretary, Millie Capri, checked her watch and said, "You're back early. Would you like me to have your lunch delivered now?"

Over the years, Mason had been asked several times why his secretary looked like a cuddly grandmother. She was in her late sixties, but didn't believe in cosmetic surgery or excessive dieting. She was comfortably round without being an unhealthy weight, and her hair was a shocking natural salt-and-pepper bob. To Mason, she was perfect. There was no temptation to sleep with her, and she was consistently, unwaveringly professional. He knew next to nothing about her personal life, and she didn't ask him about his.

Which made what he said next even more confusing to him. "I'm not hungry, so it doesn't matter when. But I do have a question. What is a respectably sized diamond for an engagement ring?"

Millie raised one eyebrow, but the rest of her expression gave nothing away. "For your income bracket? Two carats. Flawless. More than that is gaudy. Less says you're cheap."

"I need one by Friday."

"I'll have a jeweler bring samples by this afternoon. What ring size?"

Mason scratched his chin thoughtfully. "I don't know. She's petite."

"A little loose is better than too tight. I'll have him bring a range. If you find out the size, tell me, and I'll forward that information to him before he comes."

Mason started walking toward his office. He stopped and glanced back. Millie was already working on her computer again. "You're not curious why I need a ring so quickly?"

Millie looked up from her work for a moment. "Should I be?"

Mason hesitated. He had cultivated a perfectly functional impersonal work relationship with Millie. There was no reason to muddle that, but there was a question eating at him that could not be contained. "Do you think a woman would have to be insane to want to marry me?"

Millie removed her glasses and let them fall on the chain around her neck. "Senator Thorne, I think people have to be insane to want to marry at all, but it stops very few from taking that leap."

He couldn't believe he didn't know the answer to his next question. "Are you married?"

Millie held up her left hand. There was a small diamond ring next to a simple gold band. "Thirty-nine blissful years last January. We raised three boys together. Five grandchildren so far and another on the way."

Mason looked around the office. "Why don't you have any pictures of them on your desk?"

"I used to have several in the beginning. They seemed to make you uncomfortable, so I took them home."

Mason nodded. He didn't like to think he was that transparent when it came to his feelings about family, but there was no use denying it. "I appreciate that. Hold my calls for an hour. I need to read over Vine's bill proposal. He won't back mine unless I endorse his. He's a wordy bastard, though, and tends to throw in last-minute game-changing clauses. Oh . . . and if you see Andrew come through, send him in. Also, contact Liz at Shimmer and inform her that I'll be bringing a date to the event. And book the presidential suite at Milo's for the weekend under the name of Chelle Landon, but bill it to me." He spelled Chelle's name for her.

"I'll get to that immediately." He didn't doubt that she would. Millie was so good at her job that her duties extended beyond those of her job description. He was a man who trusted very few people, but Millie was one of them. He could have a team of people organizing his career and his calendar, but he preferred his life uncluttered.

Mason walked into his office and closed the door behind him. He sat at his desk and took a moment to look around. He didn't have a single photo on the wall or anywhere else. In fact, he hadn't changed a thing since he'd moved into the office six years earlier. After his first successful term, Millie had joked that he should settle into the office. He considered himself settled. At least, as much as he'd ever been.

He didn't get attached to many people or places. He took his role in California's legislature seriously, but nothing was forever. His legacy would be the bills he pushed through that would benefit his constituents and the state as a whole. He was presently working on an environmental bill that wasn't popular, but it would help protect and increase his state's water supply. Short-term solutions were Band-Aids. What they needed was funding for widespread, creative solutions. If cities could be made in deserts, then he could stop his state from doing the reverse.

He wasn't liked in certain circles lately, but that didn't bother him much. He had a handful of friends. Their opinions mattered, but even then, he did as he pleased.

Charles wasn't going to be happy when he heard that Chelle was coming to California. *Might as well face that and get it over with.* He called Charles and, after a brief exchange, said, "I thought you should hear it first from me that Chelle is coming to Sacramento."

"The same Chelle I asked you to stay away from?"

"Yep."

Charles sighed. "What are you doing, Mason? She's not your type."

"She called me and said she wanted to visit. The next thing I knew I was asking her to pretend to still be engaged to me. I don't have much more of a defense than that."

"That's no defense at all."

"Exactly. So yell at me. Be pissed. I'd like to tell you I know what I'm doing, but I'd rather be honest. I want to see her again, Charles. It's as simple as that."

"Are you looking for my permission? Because you're not going to get it. This has disaster written all over it. Chelle is as sweet and inno-cent as they come."

"And I'm what?"

"Angry. Bitter. Mason, you're talking to someone who knows you. The past has a stranglehold on you, and as long as it does, you don't have anything to give anyone."

"Then it's a wonder we're friends."

"I mean with women. I'm not a psychologist, but—"

"Then don't try to be one. Listen, I called you because I respect our friendship enough to not want this to come between us. But I don't need advice from someone who has always been as fucked up as I am."

"I'm not like that anymore, Mason. I've made peace with the past. Can you say the same?"

Mason hung up instead of answering.

He turned his cell phone in his hand and thought about Chelle. *Maybe Charles is right and I have nothing to give her. This is about nothing more than getting her into my bed. A better man would call her and tell her not to come.*

But I won't.

Chapter Six

Friday was a day of firsts. First plane ride. First limo. First time out of Texas. Chelle smoothed her hands over the skirt of the dark-blue sundress Sarah had assured her would fit in anywhere. The limo driver spoke to one of the attendants, and her luggage was whisked away. A man in a dark suit walked up to her and introduced himself as the hotel manager.

"Welcome, Miss Landon. My name is Julian. It'll be my pleasure to escort you to our presidential suite. If there is anything you need during your stay, do not hesitate to request me personally."

Chelle shook his hand while taking in the elegance of the hotel and the expensive clothing on the people entering and exiting around them. It took her a moment to register what he'd said. "There is something. This has been a mistake. I didn't request a suite. I'm only one person. And I'm not even that picky. Any room will do."

The man referred to a paper in his hand. "The reservation was made in your name by Senator Thorne. We are at full capacity this weekend, or I would offer you another room. I'm sorry." He turned and led her through a door that was held open for them by another man. "Follow me, please. I'm sure you'll find the accommodations to your satisfaction."

Once inside the elevator, Chelle said, "I'm paying for this room myself. Can I ask how much it is a night?"

Blandly, the man stated a sum that was a fourth of Chelle's savings. She gasped and leaned back against one side of the elevator. "Oh. That's not good."

Sympathy warmed what had, until that moment, been a professionally blank expression on the man's face. "Senator Thorne is a valued guest here. I am quite sure the bill will be added to his account."

With her head still spinning from the amount they charged for the suite each night, Chelle said, "I can't let him do that."

"May I humbly suggest that you settle into the suite and ring Senator Thorne regarding your concerns? Refreshments are already waiting for you. Would you like someone to unpack your luggage?"

"No, thank you," Chelle answered absently when the elevator opened right into an enormous, well-lit suite that was all glass and white furniture. Chelle heard her mother's voice in her head telling her not to touch anything. She followed the hotel manager into the suite. There was a dining room, where small sandwiches and fruit had been set out for her. A double door opened to a huge bedroom. Floor-to-ceiling windows revealed an extensive balcony with a swimming pool. She knew her jaw was hanging open, but she couldn't help it. She knew such lavish places existed, but she never thought she'd stay in one.

Chelle dug through her purse and pulled out five dollars. She handed it to the manager. He looked as if he were momentarily torn between being offended or amused. Chelle shot him a pleading smile. "Thank you for your patience with me. This is my first trip—anywhere. I don't know if I'm excited or terrified."

The man graciously pocketed her tip and handed her a business card. "This is my main number. As I said, if you need anything at all, please call me first."

Chelle looked out the window and saw the statehouse. "No wonder Mason stays here often—it's so close to where he works. I thought he lived in Sacramento, though. Why would he need to sleep here?" She looked to the manager for confirmation, but his expression had wiped itself clean. He asked her if she was all set. When she said she was, he excused himself.

Alone, Chelle walked from room to room, running her hand over the smooth white marble of the tables. *This place costs more than my car. I'm definitely not staying.* She threw open the balcony doors, stepped out onto the balcony, and smiled into the sunshine. *But there's nothing wrong with taking a moment to enjoy it.* She let her imagination go, and the balcony was suddenly full of beautifully dressed couples. She adopted an English accent and a pretentious tone. "Welcome to the presidential suite. Have I stayed here before? I practically live here, darling."

"Then you should feel right at home," Mason said from behind her.

Chelle spun, tripped over her own feet, bounced off the edge of the door, and landed in a sprawl before him, half in and half out of the doorway. She scrambled to her feet and adjusted her dress, trying to look as if she hadn't just wounded both her elbow and her pride. She waved a hand in the air. "I was joking with my guests." When that sounded crazy even to her own ears, she added, "In my head. Imagining if I had some. But I don't. And I know that." She stopped and tucked her flying curls behind her ears. "So, hi. I didn't hear you come in."

She couldn't tell if he had a huge smile on his face because he was genuinely happy to see her or because he was doubting her sanity and humoring her. "I meant to meet you at the airport, but a last-minute meeting called me in." He stepped closer to her and touched her arm gently. "You're bleeding."

Chelle pulled her arm away from him, raised her elbow, and swore. She rushed past Mason in search of tissues, but couldn't find any. What kind of hotel didn't have a visible box? She located her makeup bag and applied a Band-Aid to her small cut. It was only then she noted the drops of blood that traced her path through the suite. "Oh no."

Mason was beside her instantly. "Are you okay?"

Chelle shook her head sadly. "I was hoping to leave before they charged either one of us for the suite, but I don't know if that can happen now. I'm sure the cleaning fee for a place like this is also insane."

Mason tipped her chin up so she met his eyes. "They'll simply add it to my account. Are you okay?"

Being so close to Mason made mundane topics like her throbbing elbow easy to forget. On the flight over, she'd wondered if she had imagined how beautiful he was. She hadn't. Strong jaw, broad shoulders, eyes so blue they were mesmerizing. *No wonder I made a fool of myself over him at the wedding. Holy crap.* "I'm fine," Chelle said in a husky tone. "I can't stay here, Mason. I can't afford this."

He ran a thumb gently over her jaw. "I don't expect you to. You're here as my fiancée, remember?"

"Fake fiancée," Chelle added. It was an important distinction to keep clear in her head, especially while she fought a strong desire to throw herself into his arms and beg him to take her.

He lowered his head until his lips hovered above hers. "No one knows that but us."

Chelle licked her bottom lip and fought back a panic. She wasn't supposed to feel this strongly toward him. She was supposed to play things cool, possibly meet someone through him. Have fun. The all-consuming desire coursing through her scared her as much as it excited her. *A kiss to him is nothing more than a handshake. Don't be an idiot and read anything more into this. This is supposed to be an adventure for me and helpful to him. Breathe.* "Do you really think people will believe that we're engaged? It's not like I have a ring."

Mason dropped his hand from her face. A second later, he took her left hand in his and slid a stunning emerald-cut diamond solitaire onto her finger. "There wasn't time to have one designed for you, but this should do, and it fits."

Chelle held her shaking hand up, and the diamond mockingly sparkled at her. Panic rose within her. "I can't wear this. What if I lose it?"

He smiled down at her. "You won't."

Chelle went to pull it off. "I couldn't afford to replace it if something happened to it."

He took her hands in his. "You worry too much."

Chelle's next protest dissolved before she spoke it. Melanie and Sarah described Mason as a shameless flirt, but there was an emotion in Mason's eyes and a seriousness Chelle hadn't expected when she'd agreed to the visit. She would have sworn on her life that in this moment, he wanted her as much as she wanted him. *I've been down this road before, and it ends with abrupt and painful disappointment. He doesn't care about me. This is about the charity event. That's why he asked me here. Don't let those heavenly eyes fool you twice.* The ring was nothing more than a prop for that event. "I guess I can wear it for a day or two, just to prove we're together."

His gaze was unrelenting. "How is your elbow?"

"My elbow?"

"You hurt it," he said in a tone laced with humor.

Chelle swallowed hard. "Oh. Yes. It's fine. Just a little cut."

"I'm glad." He lowered his head again until his breath felt as soft as a caress across Chelle's parted lips. "I want to take you out tonight, and people will expect us to be comfortable doing this." His mouth claimed hers. His tongue slid teasingly between her lips. Just enough to have her part them in a gasp of wonder. It was a kiss unlike any she'd experienced before. He didn't take; he invited. He didn't plunder; he explored. He dug his hands into the hair on either side of her head and held her there gently while his tongue danced intimately with hers. When he raised his head, he was smiling. "We'll be convincing."

Convincing? Oh my God, I almost forgot why I'm here. She pushed away from him and took several deep breaths. She looked down at the ring on her finger. *It's a prop. I'm a prop. He's an actor, and this is his stage.* She glanced around the suite again. What had felt like a dream a moment before was suddenly muddled. "Why do you have an account at a hotel next to where you work?" When Mason didn't answer, Chelle met his eyes again. He gave her an odd look that birthed Chelle's next question. "Do you bring women here? Like on a regular basis?"

He shrugged. "What do you want me to say, Chelle?"

"The truth." Shaking her head, Chelle pointed to the bedroom. "Have you had sex with someone on that bed? The bed I was going to sleep in tonight?"

His answer was a slight incline of the head.

Chelle looked down at the couch beside her, and an image of him with a woman flew into her head. "And this couch? Did you christen that, too?" *I am so glad I didn't sit down.*

He raised and lowered one eyebrow in concession.

She glanced out the door at the pool she had adored only a short while earlier. "And the pool?"

He nodded.

"Are you sure you didn't miss a spot? How about where I'm standing?"

A shameless smile tugged at one corner of his mouth. He was guilty as charged, and for some reason Chelle couldn't remain irritated with him. She swore to herself in that moment she wouldn't sleep with him, but she found herself smiling back at him. "I don't feel so bad now about getting a little blood on the carpet. It sounds to me like this place is due for a little sanitizing."

Mason looked around and conceded, "I probably should have chosen a different hotel."

Chelle rolled her eyes. "You think? You don't put your fiancée in the same hotel room where you slept with everyone else. Oh my God, I don't want to know what the manager was thinking when he showed me around." Chelle waved a finger at him. "This is so wrong. One day you'll be grateful you test-drove being engaged with me, because any self-respecting woman who was actually with you would be on the first plane out of here." She looked down at the couch and wrinkled her nose at it. "I'm not staying in this room."

"I offered you a bedroom at my apartment. You said no."

"Because I didn't want to . . ."

"Sleep with me?" he asked with that sexy, coaxing tone that made her want to rip off her clothes and offer herself to him as an afternoon snack.

Friends. We're friends. Don't forget that. Chelle folded her arms across her chest. "If you really want me to stay for the weekend, you have to stop doing that."

The naughty smile was back. "Doing what?"

She waved at his smile and the expression on his face. "Constantly flirting with me. I didn't come here to sleep with you, and you seem to have plenty on your plate as far as that is concerned anyway. When we're in public, we can pretend to be together. But when we're alone, tone it down a notch. Treat me like any of your other friends who are women."

Mason scratched his chin thoughtfully. "I have sex with my female friends."

Chelle rolled her eyes. "Of course you do." It was almost funny. Almost. "There must be some woman in your life you spend time with and don't bring here."

"My secretary, Millie."

"Okay, that's promising."

"She's in her late sixties."

Chelle burst out laughing. "You have a problem."

Mason's cheeks reddened. "Ouch. Criticism from a twenty-five-year-old virgin. We could discuss what defines a healthy sex life, but you'd have to have one to contribute."

Chelle raised her hand to deliver a smack she wholeheartedly felt he deserved. He caught her hand midswing.

The air between them was instantly charged with a sexual tension so strong it had both of them breathing heavily. "You have quite a temper for someone people describe as the sweetest woman in Texas."

"You bring out the worst in me," Chelle answered.

He leaned forward and brushed his lips lightly over hers, wiping the anger clean out of her. "I could say the same. I shouldn't have made fun of your virginity. The more I think about the fact that you've never been with anyone else, the more I like the idea."

Chelle panicked and tried to pull her hand away, but he held it firmly between them. "Let me go."

"I don't know that I can." He brushed his mouth ever so lightly over her lips again. Chelle kissed him back, unable to fully resist the lure of their attraction.

A part of her held back, though. If she gave herself over to the temptation of his kiss, there was no doubt what would come next. *Tonight could be everything I wanted at the wedding. This weekend could be a wild sexual adventure with a dab of role-playing in public. No one would need to know. If I let myself go, I could step into his life. Roll onto that bed with him. Or onto that couch.*

The couch he shared with countless other women.

No.

Chelle broke free and stepped away. "Coming here was a mistake." She went to pull off the engagement ring.

"Wait," he said firmly.

Chelle froze.

He held her hands in his again, and a dark storm raged in his eyes. "I handled this badly. Don't leave."

Chelle searched his face and said earnestly, "What are we doing? We have nothing in common. We can barely say two sentences to each other without arguing. Just when I think I know what I'm doing here, you look at me, and I get all confused. I thought you needed a fake fiancée."

A battle appeared to rage within him. "I should have been more honest. I haven't been able to get you out of my head since we met. I want you, Chelle."

Her breath left her in a whoosh. Part of her rejoiced at the news, but another part clung to anger as a last line of defense. "I suppose I should be flattered, but that adds my name to what sounds like a not-very-exclusive list." She pursed her lips, then asked, "Is there even a charity event?"

He sighed. "Yes, and having you there would help me, but it's not why I invited you. I would make your first time good, Chelle. So good."

Chelle closed her eyes for a moment and gathered her thoughts. *I want him. He wants me. God knows I'm old enough. What is stopping me?* A little voice inside her whispered, *You don't want to be blended in with all the other women he had here. You want to matter.* When she opened her eyes again, she said, "Chasing you around a wedding with a condom might have given you the wrong idea about me. I'm not that wild. There has to be at least a chance the man I finally sleep with could be the one. I don't want to be just another woman on that couch."

"Okay."

Chelle's eyes snapped to his. *Wow, he agreed to that easily. Disappointingly so.* "So I should probably fly home tonight."

"No. You came all this way. We'll find you a hotel you like, and then I'll take you to dinner."

Her mind was running in circles. *He's agreeing with me and being nice about it. So why do I want to kick him in the shin?* "If I leave now, you could find another date for tonight. I'd hate to think of you spending the night alone on my account."

"I have enough women to text that it shouldn't be a problem."

Chelle gasped, and Mason laughed.

"Chelle, I'm joking."

She glared at him, not enjoying how easy it was to imagine him with another woman or how painful it was. "It's not funny."

He ducked down, kissed her briefly, and pulled her gently into his arms. She could feel his arousal. He'd said he wanted her, and his proof was hard and throbbing against her. "No, but your expression is. You're adorable."

She met his eyes. "I don't want to be adorable."

He bent and kissed her just below her ear. "What do you want to be?"

Chelle placed her hands on his shoulders to support herself. She felt as if she were melting into him. "Irresistible."

His breath was hot on her ear. "You are."

She tightened her grip on him. *Am I? Or am I merely convenient?* "I want to say yes, Mason. Part of me says I should just let go and do this. Part of me is scared. I'm sorry I'm sending you mixed signals."

There was an expression in his eyes she couldn't decipher. "What are you afraid of?"

"I always imagined my first time would be with a man who loved me. It's strange letting go of that dream." She cringed as she said it. "I sound like an idiot."

Mason hugged her to his chest and rested his chin lightly against her forehead. "No. I'm the idiot. We need to get out of this hotel. Let's go."

She stepped back and glanced around. "What are they going to think when we ask to have my things packed up again, and they see drops of blood all over the place?"

"They've seen worse," Mason said with a twinkle in his eye.

Chelle grabbed her purse and swung it in his direction, chastising him. She couldn't tell if he was serious, but she still said, "You are so bad."

"Women love that about me." He winked at her.

Chelle led the way to the door and shook her head. She hadn't meant to voice her thoughts, but she did. "I'd need more."

"I know," Mason said so softly Chelle wasn't sure she'd heard him right. She looked back at him, but his expression gave nothing away.

What are we doing? I thought I knew, but now I'm not so sure.

One minute I want to slap Mason; the next I want to jump him.

He'd be perfectly happy showing me the joys of sex, then dropping me back at the airport on Sunday.

But I want . . .

That's the problem.

I don't know what I want.

Mason relaxed into an uncomfortable chair beside Chelle's hotel bed. She'd insisted they choose a hotel that fit her budget because she was determined to pay her own way. He hadn't stayed in a hotel room this small since . . . he couldn't remember ever staying in less than a one-bedroom suite.

The small room did have its perks. She'd had to brush against him several times as she'd unpacked and chosen her clothing for the evening. In a moment of indecision, she had held one dress up in front of her, then another, and asked him to help her choose.

He'd been tempted to say neither, close the distance between them, and help her out of her sundress, but he was still reeling from what she'd said earlier. Having her was all he'd been able to think about since she'd said she was flying out to see him, but he'd never met a woman like her before. Each time he asked himself why a woman as beautiful as Chelle would still be a virgin, he didn't like the answer. She wasn't lying when she said she wanted it to mean something. To her, sex was more than something two adults could engage in recreationally. He didn't want to be the one to disillusion her.

He thought about his first time. He had been eighteen and at the peak of his popularity. Irene had been his agent since he was seven years old. She'd gotten him movie deal after movie deal, scheduled all of his appearances, taken him from a middle-class unknown to an international household name.

He'd considered her the most beautiful woman he'd ever seen. Sophisticated. Intelligent. Untouchable. Until she'd taken him to her bed, and he'd fallen in love with her completely as only the young and foolish could do.

He hadn't understood back then that sex could be used to control someone. She'd said she loved him. With her encouragement, he'd fired his father as his manager, severed legal ties with his parents, and given her greater access to his earnings. He'd been so besotted with her that had she asked him to kill for her, he'd probably be in jail for the crime to that day.

It had taken losing his mother to a prescription drug overdose to wake him up. No one had called it a suicide, and Mason had never been quite sure himself. His father had said that she had fallen into a deep depression since her final fight with Mason. He and his father had barely spoken since.

After his mother's death, Mason had shut down, unable to work. Unable to think. When the movie he'd been working on fell behind schedule and he was threatened with lawsuits, Irene had quickly distanced herself from him, taking as much of his money with her as she could.

That had been Mason's only venture into love.

Mason's mind wandered to the dark place he'd fallen into after his mother's death. He'd partied too much and had nearly repeated his mother's tragedy more than once. It was his second stay in rehab that saved Mason. One of his counselors—he didn't remember the man's name—had turned harsh with him one day. He'd told him to stop blaming others; only he was responsible for his choices. Life could be cruel and senseless, but when people were faced with adversity, how they responded to it determined if they had what it took to survive.

"Do you want to survive, or do you want to join your mother? Take control of your life, Mason, before you lose it. No one can save you, and no one can destroy you. Only you have that power."

The counselor's words had resonated with Mason.

The next day, he had announced his retirement from the acting world and set himself free. He stopped trying to connect with his father and put aside his childhood fantasy of what family should be. He removed all expectations when it came to women. And he was happier.

His journey became about him and no one else.

Mason chose a college and created a whole new life for himself. He met Charles, and a solid friendship was born. He and Charles each wanted nothing more than to shed their past and prove to the world that they were a force to be reckoned with. Different backgrounds, different reasons, but they had more in common than either expected, and their friendship endured. Charles encouraged him to channel his anger toward causes where he could make a positive difference. While still in school, Mason lobbied for laws that would protect child actors and their assets. He encouraged Charles to put aside his middle-class, work boot–filled upbringing and act the part of the financial tycoon he'd become.

Through his causes, Mason met rich and powerful politicians and discovered they weren't all the weasels the media made them out to be. Many had chosen the career because they believed in something bigger than themselves. Politics was a game. Some played it for honorable reasons and followed the rules. Some had their own agendas and made dirty backdoor deals. Mason entered that world with his eyes already open to the ugly potential within even those who claimed to be allies, and that proved to be a strength for him.

At twenty-five, Mason had used his connections to become one of the youngest state senators in California. Although he acknowledged that his name recognition had given him an advantage, he had worked hard to prove he deserved the leadership role. He kept his energy and his goals focused on the future. He could have used his influence to track down his old agent and exact some form of revenge. A woman in her late twenties didn't sleep with a boy for the pleasure; she'd used sex to control him. Revenge, however, would mean opening a door to the past, and he had no desire to test whether it had the power to destroy him twice.

Chelle didn't have a darker side. She still believed there was some good in everyone. Faith in humanity was something that was best shed, like a child's first set of teeth. Someone would one day break Chelle's heart and teach her how little the word *love* meant, but Mason didn't want to be that person. Which didn't mean he didn't want to fuck her, but it did mean he shouldn't allow himself to. His hands clenched into fists. *I'm a mess.*

"Mason?" Chelle called out from the bathroom.

He imagined her standing there, naked and still wet from the shower. He shifted as his trousers became uncomfortably tight in the front. "Yes?"

"I forgot to grab a bra when I came in here. Do you mind handing me one through the door? They're in the top drawer of the bureau."

He looked skyward. *I'm really trying to do the right thing here.*

He pushed himself out of the chair and opened the drawer she'd directed him to. Most of her underclothing was exactly as he would have imagined. Cotton with flowers. Innocent. Off to the side was a sheer black lace bra and thong. He picked them up and groaned. They were her get-lucky set. Every woman had them. Some women wore them all the time. He took a moment to picture her wearing only that sliver of lace.

"Did you find one?" Chelle called out from the bathroom.

"Trying to decide between the daisies and the roses."

"Just grab anything. It won't matter with this dress."

Oh yes, it will.

Mason walked the black thong and bra over to the trash and almost dropped them in, but pocketed them instead. If he wasn't going to see her in them, he'd be damned if some other man would. He returned to her underwear drawer and picked out a chaste cotton bra and shook his head with amusement at it. Mason went to the door of the bathroom. "This should work," he said, both to her and to himself. If he needed to be reminded of her innocence, the flowery pattern was a modern-day chastity belt.

Chelle stuck a hand out and grabbed the bra. "Thank you. I would have come out for it, but I didn't realize I had forgotten to grab one until I was in the shower. I thought this was better than sprinting out there in just a towel."

It was painfully easy to fantasize about how Chelle would look in nothing more than a hotel towel. Mason turned on his heel and strode back across the room to where he had been sitting.

A few minutes later, Chelle entered the room in the simple black dress he'd told her he preferred. It was nice enough to be appropriate for the expensive restaurant he'd chosen, but had a high neckline and short sleeves that covered the delicate shoulders he'd spent too much time wanting to rain kisses across. She had pulled her blonde hair up into a loose knot he was more than a little tempted to release.

They stood there for a long moment lost in each other. Eventually, he broke the silence. "You clean up well."

The smile she sent his way was tentative, but warm. "I wasn't sure what to bring, but Sarah and Melanie went shopping with me for this trip. There aren't many reasons to dress up when you live and work on a ranch. It's nice to be out of jeans for once."

Your tight little ass would look amazing in jeans. Just jeans. No top. Your pert little tits puckered and eager for my mouth. Mason cleared his throat. "Are you ready? We don't want to miss our reservation. I have a car downstairs."

She picked up a small clutch bag, then they walked out of the hotel room together. They stood side by side, somewhat awkwardly, in the elevator as it descended to the lobby. He told himself to keep his hands off her, but the lure of her was too strong. He rested one hand possessively on the small of her back as they exited the elevator. That slight connection was enough to have his heart racing in his chest.

She looked up at him as if she felt the same way.

Despite his good intentions, he lowered his mouth to hers briefly, allowing him just the briefest taste of the forbidden. When he raised his head, her cheeks were flushed, and *yes* shone in her eyes. Doing the right thing had never been so hard. He gently chucked her beneath the chin and said, "I'll miss this when you're gone."

Her eyes darkened and he wanted to take the words back, but he didn't. If she knew how much he wanted her, she might waver in her decision. He needed her to be strong. If that meant denting her feelings a little, it was preferable to how hurt she'd be if she fell for a man who was incapable of loving anyone.

Why am I torturing myself by taking her to dinner?

I can't have her on her terms.

And she could never handle mine.

She smiled at him, already forgiving him and making him feel like more of an ass. He almost walked into the revolving exit door, but stopped at the last minute.

"Where are we going?" she asked.

I wish I knew.

Chapter Seven

As they walked into the restaurant Mason had chosen, Chelle stole a glance at him and wondered if he was as confused as she was. *I told him I didn't want to sleep with him, so why do I keep teasing him? Do I want him to want me so much I can't say no?*

Even if he did, how long would it last? A night? A week?

Could I handle something like that?

Mason escorted her through the restaurant, which looked very expensive. There wasn't a man in sight who wasn't wearing a tailored suit, nor was there a woman who wasn't covered with blinding diamonds. She felt underdressed, but she doubted many noticed. All eyes were on Mason. He might have an ego the size of Texas, but she could see how he'd gotten it. Women stopped talking to their dates as he walked by and became embarrassingly starstruck. Men watched him, probably wanting to be him.

I could strip naked and dance on the table, and no one would notice. It was interesting to see what was valued in Mason's world. Her father had always said a man's measure was in how he treated his family. His strength was in his dedication to them, his toughness in his ability to protect those weaker than him. But Mason was adored for his strong jawline and his athletic build. He was envied for what he had, how he looked, and the power he wielded, not necessarily the man he was. Chelle wondered if that was all that was important to him.

After their drinks and meals were ordered, Chelle met Mason's eyes across the table. He seemed oblivious to the amount of attention he was receiving from the other patrons. Of course, his first career had been on the big screen, so being the center of everyone's attention was something he'd be used to. She realized she knew very little about him outside of what he did for a living. *Or outside of hotels.* "Is your family in Sacramento, too?"

His expression turned guarded. "I don't have much family."

"What about your parents? Where do they live?"

He sat back, began to pick up a fork, then dropped it back to the table. "I'd rather hear about you. I get the sense that life on a ranch wasn't what you had planned for yourself."

Chelle wanted to push him to open up to her, but didn't. She liked to think that if they could be nothing else, they could at least be friends. Trust and friendship were two things that were best not rushed. Not with animals. Not with people. "I don't mind Fort Mavis. There's something wonderful about knowing help is never more than a holler away. I don't know what it's like to walk down a street and not know the names of everyone I come across. It's just that lately I've been thinking things could be good without being great. I might be wrong; maybe great isn't attainable. I don't know. But I started to feel trapped in my life. Sarah says I may realize there is nothing out here for me and decide that I love Fort Mavis, but I won't know for sure if I don't see what it's like outside of Texas, will I? So that's what I'm doing. I'm on an adventure."

The flirtatious Mason from before had been replaced by a serious man who looked moved by what she was saying. "Sounds like a healthy approach to figuring out what you want."

His praise warmed her heart. This wasn't the empty flattery that came so easily to him. "Thank you, although I doubt my parents agree. They're afraid I'll write home that I've joined a traveling circus."

Mason chuckled. "Do they know you're out here visiting me?" He brushed his hand over her left one. "That you're engaged?"

"No to both," Chelle said with a guilty smile. "I left out some of the details of this vacation. My parents are good people, but I'd never hear the end of it if I tried to explain this to them."

"You still live with them?"

Even though his tone hadn't been judgmental, Chelle stiffened. "I had planned to go away to school, but it wasn't meant to be." She briefly told him the story of her grandfather and how she'd stayed to care for him. "I don't regret a minute of it, though. I miss him every day. He was an open-minded man. I'd like to think he's up there cheering me on as I try to figure out what I want to do next. My parents would love to see me marry locally and take over the family ranch. I don't have the heart to tell them it's not my dream. I don't know where I'm meant to be, but have you ever gotten the feeling you're still a work in progress?" Mason was watching her so quietly Chelle started to worry she'd talked so much he'd started daydreaming. "I'm sorry, I rattle on sometimes."

Mason took her hand in his. "Don't be sorry. I enjoy listening to you. I don't know that I've ever met anyone like you. What do you consider your greatest flaw? Do you even have one?"

She made a face at his question. "Flaws? Sure. I just admitted to practically lying to my parents. I'm not perfect. No one is."

With a flash of red, a stunning, tall brunette in a dress that revealed more than it concealed interrupted them. "Senator Thorne, I didn't know you were back in town."

Mason stood to greet the woman. He offered her his hand, but she gave him a quick kiss on the cheek instead. He took his seat again and said, "Chelle, this is an old friend of mine, Cameron Linke. Cam, this is my fiancée, Chelle Landon."

The woman's jaw dropped open. "Your fiancée?"

Chelle held up her left hand and wiggled her fingers, flashing her engagement ring at her. Although Chelle felt a twinge of jealousy, based on what she guessed was the history between Mason and the woman, it was hard not to be amused by how shocked the woman looked. "It's a pleasure to meet you."

"You're really engaged?" Cam looked Chelle over, sizing her up.

Chelle smiled at her and shrugged. "It does seem that way."

The woman looked skeptical for another moment, then a smile spread across her face. She raised her hand to her ear and asked, "Do you hear that? That's the sound of a hundred single women sighing in disappointment at the news. You may have caught him, but are you sure you have what it takes to hold on to a man like this?"

Chelle met Mason's eyes across the table. Maybe it was because all of it was an act anyway, but she found it easy to banter back. "I don't worry about that. He's still working on proving he has what it takes to hold on to a woman like me." She winked at Mason for emphasis, enjoying how unexpectedly uncomfortable he looked. "But he's getting there."

Cam threw back her head and laughed. "Oh, I like you, darling. I hope it does work out for you two. You're just what he needs." With that, she excused herself and walked away.

Chelle smiled as she watched her go. She stopped, however, when she saw the expression on Mason's face. He didn't look very happy. Chelle reviewed everything she'd said. Was she coming on too strong to be believable? "Did I say something wrong? What's the matter, Mason?"

Mason wasn't a man who spent a whole lot of time analyzing how he felt. It didn't require a degree in psychology, however, to attribute the irritation he felt to the amusement in Chelle's eyes when she'd spoken to Cameron. Chelle had enjoyed the conversation because she wasn't worried about losing him.

What had she said earlier? She didn't take him seriously, and he was discovering that wasn't a feeling he enjoyed. He wanted to pull her into his arms and prove her wrong.

A month ago, Mason would have said he was living a nearly perfect life. Both his professional and his personal life were exactly the way he wanted them to be. He played by his rules, and his casual lifestyle was something he'd been proud of.

He continued to glare at her. Chelle Landon had come into his life and turned everything upside down. Since meeting her, Mason had come face-to-face with the low opinion Charles had of him. He'd realized the women who slept with him saw him as little more than a reliable screw. Instead of reveling in the freedom that gave him, he resented how easily they all dismissed him as a potential life partner.

He was no one's joke.

He'd felt like this once before. After he'd walked off the set of a movie because he'd still been reeling from his mother's death and Irene had stopped taking his calls. He'd begged her not to leave him, but she'd explained that she could never have feelings for someone half her age. She'd told him to grow up and realize sex was just that—sex. The sting of her rejection had echoed through him when Chelle had joked about him not being good enough for her.

Chelle put her hand on his tense one. "I don't understand why you're upset, but I want to."

The softness of her tone, the sincerity in her eyes brought him back to the present. He laced his fingers with hers. "Sorry. I haven't eaten anything yet today, and hunger puts me in a foul mood." He beamed a smile at her in an attempt to distract her.

She looked down at their linked hands, then back up to his eyes. "Just so you know, I'm really good at knowing when people are lying to me. I'll let you get away with it this time, though."

He marveled at how quickly he could go from feeling defensive and angry to once again being completely mesmerized by Chelle's voice. He neither agreed nor disagreed with her.

Her smile was gentle and accepting as she continued, "New friendships are tough, aren't they? Deciding what to share and what to hide? You don't have to tell me anything. It might not be worth it. Really, after tomorrow, how much will we see each other? Unless you think we could be friends, and then I'd say honesty is a good foundation for that."

Mason tightened his fingers on hers. "I don't know if I've ever actually been friends with a woman. Not by your definition, anyway."

Chelle cocked her head to one side. "Maybe it's time you change that."

Their food arrived, and they both took a moment to savor the steak. Mason had called it chateaubriand, and it came with béarnaise sauce. Chelle claimed to be hard to impress because she came from cattle country where steaks were plentiful, but he smiled when she said it was melt-in-your-mouth wonderful. Mason could have let the topic from earlier drop. Chelle wasn't pushing him to open up to her, but somehow that made him want to. "I learned some tough lessons at the end of my acting career. I usually consider them ancient history, but sometimes I have flashbacks to moments that would be better forgotten."

Chelle nodded quietly.

When she didn't push for more, he asked, "You're not going to ask for details?"

She shook her head. "My mother would say, 'You can yell for the sun to come up in the middle of the night and be angry when it doesn't, or you can wait for things to happen as they're supposed to.'"

The more Mason thought about that advice, the more he liked it. It didn't fit, though, with his first impression of Chelle. "You're much more levelheaded than you came across at the wedding."

Chelle glanced away and laughed self-consciously. "Yeah, that wasn't me at my best. I guess you could say I saw the sun setting and went scrambling after it by throwing myself at you."

The way she shared her own insecurity as if it were the most natural thing to do crumbled another wall around Mason's heart. He took her hand in his again. "The sun is far from setting on you."

Chelle met his eyes and shrugged awkwardly. "I try to tell myself that, but it's getting harder and harder to believe. That's why I'm here. I don't want to wake up and realize I let life pass me by."

Mason wasn't sure if she was referring to traveling, losing her virginity, or both. He was torn between demanding that she keep waiting and offering to show her what she'd been missing. Neither felt like the right thing to do, so he said, "You asked me about my family. I haven't spoken to my father in well over ten years. He used to be my manager when I was an actor. That was a difficult situation. Children want to please their parents, and I wanted mine to be proud, but I also wanted to control my own career. I fired my father when I turned eighteen. That didn't go over very well. My mother overdosed on prescription drugs a short time later, and my life pretty much went to shit for a year after that. When you're at the top, everyone loves you. It's a whole other story when things go south. That's when you discover who your real friends are, if you have any. And I didn't. Chelle, you might feel like you've missed out, but I've been in life's fast lane for as long as I can remember, and there's a price to be paid for that, too. Hang on to your innocence as long as you can. The world out here can get ugly."

No actress could have copied the sweet look of concern on Chelle's face. Expressions like that came from the heart. Chelle had a softer one than anyone he'd ever met. "I'm so sorry to hear about your mother. That must have been horrible. I don't know your father to know what would keep him away, but I'd bet he's hurting about it just as much as you are." Chelle gave his hand a tight squeeze. "Mason Thorne, the more I get to know you, the more I like you."

Mason frowned and said nothing. He absently played with the diamond ring on her left hand. *That's the same problem I'm having.*

Chapter Eight

The next night Chelle, was standing in front of her cell phone doing a little spin in her flirty little black dress. "So do you approve?"

Sarah exclaimed from afar, "Yes! The dress is perfect. I love your hair up like that. You look so happy, too."

Chelle smiled into the phone. Video chat was a beautiful thing. "I am. You were right. This is the adventure I needed. Mason took me to dinner last night. Tonight we're off to a charity dinner. I'm having fun."

Sarah leaned closer to the camera on her phone and said, "I can't believe you're out there pretending to be engaged to Mason. I mean, I know I suggested you do it, but it still sounds crazy when I say it. What's it like?"

Chelle picked up the phone so Sarah could stay with her as she checked her makeup in the hotel bathroom. "It's interesting. People tend to be really surprised when they first hear that Mason and I are engaged, but then they take the news well."

With wide eyes, Sarah said, "The way Mason goes through women, I was afraid your visit would be one catfight after another. Nothing like that?"

"No. Not so far."

"So you're staying in a hotel alone? And nothing is . . . going on between you two?"

"Are you asking me if I slept with him?"

Sarah laughed. "Yes."

"I didn't. And I don't think it's going to happen."

"You sound disappointed."

There was no reason to lie. Sarah wasn't the type to judge. "I'm not. Well, not really. It's hard to explain. I like him—so much more than I thought I would. On the outside he's all flirt and swagger, but on the inside there is someone who has been really hurt. He was telling me about his family, and I wanted to hug him and say everything was going to be okay."

"That doesn't sound like the Mason I know."

"It's not the Mason I thought I was coming to visit. I came because I thought it would be exciting, but it's so much more than that."

Sarah wiped one of her cheeks. "That's so beautiful."

Chelle found her own eyes misting up. "You're a cornball. Stop, before I mess up my makeup."

"Promise to call me tomorrow and tell me every last detail about your date tonight."

"It's not a date. He said this might help him get support for his bill."

Sarah laughed. "You keep telling yourself that. Oh, and remember, even though you'll be meeting dignitaries and people who could probably buy and sell Texas, don't let them intimidate you. They have more money and power than you, but that doesn't make them better than you."

Chelle froze. "I wasn't even worried about that until you just said it."

Sarah shook her head back and forth with a huge apologetic smile. "Oh, then Etch A Sketch it right out of your head."

Chelle checked her makeup in a hand mirror. "I'll try."

"I miss you," Sarah said with a huge smile.

"Me too," Chelle admitted. She thought about what Mason had said about not having friends when he was younger and felt doubly blessed to have so many. "Tell Melanie I miss her, too."

"I will," Sarah answered and hung up.

A few minutes later, Chelle jumped at a knock at the door. She opened it and tried not to dissolve into an adoring pool at Mason's feet. He was far too handsome on a regular day, but in formal attire he was drop dead gorgeous. He leaned in to give her a kiss on the cheek, and she inhaled deeply. He smelled as good as he looked.

Friends. Just friends.

Mason's lips lingered on Chelle's cheek longer than he'd intended. He lifted his head and looked down into her eyes. Innocent desire burned within them and shook his resolve. She looked as hungry to kiss him as he was to kiss her.

Friends. Just friends, he reminded himself harshly. "You look beautiful."

"You too," she answered in a rush, then blushed.

This is hell. Mason stepped back from her. "Are you ready?"

She nodded wordlessly and walked with him out the door and to the elevator. He offered her his arm, and she linked hers with his as naturally as if they'd known each other for years. When they stepped out of the elevator door, she tugged on his sleeve as if she wanted to say something to him. He bent and she turned in his arms and gave him a deep kiss that sent him rocking back onto his heels. Her tongue swept through his mouth, flirting with his, but withdrawing before he had time to respond. Mason stared at her, feeling dazed.

Chelle said softly, "For the sake of those watching."

Mason swallowed hard. He could barely breathe, but he said, "Good thinking," in the calmest voice he could muster.

He was still working on calming his libido when they slid into the backseat of the car he'd hired for the night. She turned half away from him and asked, "I thought I'd brought underwear to match this dress, but I couldn't find it anywhere. Is the strap of my bra showing?"

Mason wasn't admitting to anything. "It's fine."

She sat back with a smile. "Oh good. I could have sworn I remembered unpacking them. But I guess I didn't. Strange, huh?"

He loosened the tie that suddenly felt tight around his neck. "Yesterday was a busy day." Which wasn't a lie.

Chelle looked out the window briefly, then met his eyes again. Her cheeks were glowing with excitement. "This weekend is flying by. I can't believe I leave tomorrow. I feel like I just got here."

"Are you heading home?"

"I considered that, but instead I'm going to do something completely spontaneous."

Mason couldn't have looked away from Chelle if he'd tried. "What?"

"Sarah already helped me arrange it. I'm not deciding my next destination until I get to the airport." She briefly described the box Sarah had made with all the photos glued to cards. "Sarah will pull out a card, and whatever place is on it, that's where I'm headed next."

"And then?"

Chelle's confidence wavered for just a second, but she continued on in a gush of enthusiasm. "It depends. This is a journey as much as it is a vacation. Sarah says you have to trust fate to take you where you belong. It worked for her, so I'm giving it a try—at least until my savings run out." She chewed her bottom lip. "I know that sounds a little irresponsible, but like I said, I'm a work in progress."

Mason touched the side of her face gently before forcing himself to break the connection. Being with Chelle felt good. Too good. He wanted her to find where she belonged and didn't want to be what stood in her way. Still, the idea of not seeing her again was hard to accept. "Keep me updated on where you decide to go."

She gave him a cautious sideways look. "You really want to know?"

He surprised himself by not retracting the idea. "I don't like the idea of you traveling alone."

That brought a smile to her face. "Now you sound like David."

Wham. Mason's mood took a jealous turn. "What did he think of you coming here to see me?"

"He didn't ask, and I didn't say. He's been moody ever since he heard Lucy got engaged. No one blames him. It was unexpected, to say the least. If you ask my opinion, he fell in love with her when he went out there to see her and was too damn stubborn to tell her. Texan men can be loyal to the grave, but try getting one of them to talk about their feelings. My first boyfriend wrote a love song for me in high school. Or that's what he said it was. It was all about his truck and how much he liked driving it. That's probably why I never slept with him. I didn't want to compete with a vehicle."

Neither David nor the boyfriend she referenced sounded like men she had any sexual interest in, but the thought of Chelle being with anyone was enough to send Mason's thoughts on dark tangents. Was Chelle heading off to parts unknown looking for a husband, a new career, or something a bit more carnal?

That thought alone made him want to demand she go home.

He'd always considered monogamy an archaic practice, but when he was with Chelle he felt territorial in a way he'd never been. He'd never cared who a woman was with before or after him.

Chelle was different. He wanted to be her first and her last lover. It was an admission that shook him to the core.

"Who was your first girlfriend?" Chelle surprised him by asking.

Mason forced himself to focus on her question and not on his primitive desire to pound his chest and claim her as his. "I didn't date much until college. My acting career started early, and then travel and long days of filming kept me away from people my age. People wonder why so many children who make it in Hollywood end up in rehab. I don't. It's a lifestyle no one can prepare you for. One day you're playing street hockey with your neighborhood friends, just being a regular kid. The next day everyone knows you, and you're expected to navigate situations and make decisions that would intimidate most adults. You can never have a normal day again. People equate money and fame with happiness, so you don't find much sympathy if you get to the top and wonder if what you lost was worth it. You will never meet someone without wondering if they like you just for you or for what you can do for them. You're always watched. Always judged. It's easy to feel trapped."

"Did you feel that way?" Chelle asked, laying a gentle hand on one of his thighs.

He covered her hands with one of his own. "I did and made a lot of bad choices because of it."

The squeeze she gave his thigh was meant to be reassuring. It wasn't supposed to send his blood rushing downward to his overly eager cock.

"You were so young. And then you lost your mother. You're allowed a few mistakes."

In all the years that had passed since that time, Mason hadn't shared his story with anyone besides Charles. For a reason he couldn't explain to himself, he wanted Chelle to see him for who he was. "That time in my life changed me, Chelle. Not necessarily in a good way."

Chelle's eyes flew to his. "Why does that sound like a warning?"

He laced his fingers with hers. "There's something between you and me. I know you feel it, too. We'd be good together, Chelle, until you realized I can't be the man you're looking for."

Chelle looked down at their linked hands. "And what do you think that is?"

He watched her expression closely as he said, "A dependable husband. Someone with a nine-to-five job. A father for children you've probably already named. Someone who will want to live happily ever after with you in Fort Mavis."

Chelle whistled softly, and she looked as though she felt a little sick. "Wow. Here I was thinking I needed to figure out what to do with my life because I didn't know, but thank God you have a whole future planned out for me."

He searched her face and was about to say more, but they arrived at the governor's home. The driver opened the door and helped Chelle out. Mason took his place beside her. He could feel the tension in her back. "We don't have to go in."

The smile on her face seemed forced for the benefit of those watching them walk into the event. "I'm fine. I'm merely amazed how little you know me."

He took her elbow in one of his hands and pulled her closer. "I'm not judging your decisions."

Her beautiful eyes met his solemnly. "What are you so afraid of, Mason?"

His hand tightened on her elbow. "I don't want to hurt you."

She laid a hand on his cheek and said softly, "Then don't."

He covered her hand with his. "It's not that simple."

He felt her smile before he saw it.

"My father would say, 'Life is only as complicated as you make it.'"

"No offense, but I don't want to think about your father right now," Mason growled softly. He bent and kissed her, forgetting about the press that was gathered at the entrance of the charity event.

The moment was broken by photographers closing in and some of the press calling out questions to them. "Senator Thorne, why the fast engagement?" "Who is she?" "Have you chosen a wedding date?" "Senator Thorne, is it true you were considering running for governor but were warned that your image needed to be whitewashed? Is that why you're getting married?" "Senator Thorne, what does Ruby Skye think of your engagement?"

Mason turned to the press with a forced natural smile. Ruby was an old friend from his acting days. They hadn't slept together in years, but Ruby still sometimes called when she needed a date who wouldn't read anything into the invitation, someone who could handle himself in front of cameras. The press had linked them as a couple as many times as they'd written fictional accounts of them breaking up. The truth was Mason only helped Ruby because he understood why she needed to sometimes be with someone who expected nothing from her.

Mason didn't argue with the press. He wrapped an arm around Chelle and stood proudly beside her. Paparazzi didn't care about the truth. They wanted a good story. It was better to give them a sound bite than to leave them floundering and creating their own. "My fiancée was born and raised in a small town in Texas. She looks sweet, but her best friend is the Takedown Cowgirl, and we all know not to mess with her. Chelle Landon has stolen my heart and is hell-bent on reforming me. Let's give her time to settle in before scaring her with stories of how monumental that feat will be." He winked at just the right moment and was rewarded with an audible sigh from the female reporters.

Mason glanced down at Chelle to make sure she was okay and was pleasantly surprised with how she handled herself before the cameras. She didn't know the press well enough to understand how quickly they could turn on her, but that was another lesson he hoped she wouldn't learn from her time with him. He and Chelle stood for several photos before turning to continue their walk into the event.

One of the reporters yelled out, "Ms. Landon, do you really think you can reform one of California's most notorious bachelors?"

Chelle looked over her shoulder at the reporter and beamed at him. "With love, anything is possible." With her down-home tone, she won over the crowd as easily as he ever had. They were snapping her photo and smiling back at her. He doubted there would be a local station that didn't run a photo or video clip of them together.

Together.

Mason's throat tightened, and he found it impossible to breathe for a heartbeat. He knew she was acting. Like him, she was saying what the press wanted to hear and keeping their charade believable. So why did he feel like a man who'd received a sucker punch?

Wanting to sleep with Chelle was one thing, but watching her handle the media with ease, then turn and smile at him as if it were the most natural thing left him shaking in his Brooks Brothers. *She isn't supposed to fit here. Being with her shouldn't feel this right.*

Mason spent the next three hours watching Chelle win over everyone she met. She appeared to sincerely enjoy meeting new people and did so with a grace she'd hidden well the first time he'd met her. She chatted easily with the wives and joked with the husbands in a non-threatening way that put both at ease.

When Senator Goss joined them, Mason was tempted to warn her to keep her jokes to a minimum. Goss was as starched stiff as they came. He'd had it out for Mason ever since Mason's freshman year in the senate when Mason had accidentally slept with the wife of the majority floor leader. The woman had told Mason she was single. The truth was she and her husband were separated, and she'd been looking for a way to pay him back for his own infidelity. The truth hadn't mattered. The story of how Mason had broken up a marriage within six months of being in office had laid the foundation for how his fellow senators saw him.

Chelle flashed her sweetest smile at Senator Goss and complimented him on receiving an award that had made the news. That one comment seemed to win Goss over. He asked her about her home in Texas, and she told him about Fort Mavis. In a span of only a few minutes, Chelle had Goss doing something Mason had never seen—smiling.

"I grew up in a small town, too," the older senator said in gruff approval. "Thorne, you've got a good woman here."

Mason put his arm around Chelle's waist lightly. "I'm aware of that."

Goss waved a stern finger at Chelle. "What does your father think of Thorne?"

Even though Mason knew Chelle's answer would be a fabrication, he found he wanted to hear it. She glanced up at Mason with an adoration that started his heart pounding painfully in his chest. She deepened her usually light drawl for effect and said, "My father should have been born in Missouri. He's a 'show me' kind of man. If Mason is good to me, my father will come round. If Mason's not, don't worry; we'll bury him real quiet like." She voiced the threat with an angelic smile that won a loud laugh from Senator Goss.

With a nod of approval, the senator said, "Thorne, if you marry this one, I may have to change my opinion of you. She sees something in you. I hope she's right."

Normally, Mason would have answered with a sarcastic retort that would have set Goss back a step, but instead he met Chelle's guileless gaze and said, "I hope so, too."

Chelle blushed beneath the attention and looked away. He wanted to tell her it was all for show, but he wasn't sure it was.

His mother had been high-strung and emotional. He'd loved her, but being around her had always been difficult. One misplaced word had been enough to set her off. His father had taken care of her the best he could, but he wouldn't have described his mother as a strong woman.

Not like Chelle.

The more he learned about her, the more he understood how she had gotten to twenty-five without sleeping with a man. She had definite ideas about how things ought to be and wasn't influenced by fear of what others thought of her. He had the sinking feeling he was in the presence of what, at least in his experience, was a rare find—a genuinely good person.

A woman like that has no business with a man like me.

Later that night, Chelle rode up the elevator of her hotel beside a pensive Mason. Although they had successfully convinced everyone at the charity event, including the attending press, that they were engaged, Mason didn't look happy. They had ridden back from the event in relative silence, a state that had given her far too much time to think.

She stole a glance at Mason's profile. How could someone who had everything sometimes look so lost? Turn a camera on Mason and his smile alone could melt his opposition; he was simply that good-looking. Add money and a dash of fame, and he was living most people's fantasy life. So why did he look tormented when he thought no one was watching? What dark thoughts haunted him?

She'd spent the evening torn between wanting him physically and wanting to comfort him. It took only the slightest touch from him anywhere on her body to set her on fire. She craved to feel that way again, to know what pleasure could be found beyond their light kisses.

What if he's the only one who makes me feel this way? How can I walk away from a chance to taste real passion? I know I said I wanted to wait to be with someone who might matter, but how could anything that feels this good be wrong?

Chelle slid her hand into his and gave it a squeeze. He looked down at her, and his nostrils flared as he seemed to read her thoughts. She sent him a mental message: *I don't want to fight this anymore. Take me.*

The elevator door opened, and they walked to the door of her hotel room. Chelle dropped his hand to find the key card to her door. She swiped it, opened the door, then sought his eyes again. "Mason?"

He raised a hand to cup one side of her face. His jaw was tight with determination. "You did well tonight, Chelle. My bill may just pass, and I'll have you to thank. You brought over a few votes tonight that have opposed me in the past simply out of spite. I bet you didn't realize politics was so much like high school."

Chelle was finding it hard to concentrate on anything beyond the way his lips moved as he spoke. She imagined how they'd feel inching their way down her neck. How his strong hands would feel as they pushed the fabric of her dress aside, giving his mouth access to more of her, to as much of her as he wanted. "I'm glad I could help."

He ran a thumb softly over her parted lips. "Don't look at me like that, Chelle. There is only one way kissing you would end."

"Would that be such a bad thing?" she murmured.

He groaned. "We both know you want—"

Chelle grabbed Mason by the tie and pulled his face down to just above hers. She threw her arms around his neck and whispered, "This is what I want."

She closed the short distance between their lips and kissed him with all the desire that had been building up within her since the first moment she'd met him. Her body melted against his. Their kiss deepened hungrily, desperately.

Mason swung her up into his arms and kicked the hotel door shut behind him. He lowered her to her feet beside the bed. "I can't promise you forever. Or even next week. Nothing we said today was true. I need to know you understand that."

His blue eyes darkened with emotion, and his concern for her had the opposite effect he was hoping for. Mason cared about her. No matter what he said, he was clearly giving her another chance to leave, trying to protect her from what he thought would hurt her. What he didn't understand was that she would never regret being with him, even if she woke up alone. Before him, she hadn't known it was possible to want a man so intensely that pride fell away. The real tragedy would be not how quickly he left her, but how sad her life would have been had he never shown her she was right to want more.

"You do a lot of talking for a man who says he's so good in bed." Chelle unzipped the back of her dress and let it drop to the floor around her. She stood there proudly in her chaste cotton bra and panties, glorying in the knowledge that what he wanted had nothing to do with what she was wearing. She unsnapped her bra and dropped it beside her. Without breaking eye contact, she stepped out of her high heels and slid off her panties. She stood before him, nude and amazingly unafraid.

He raised a hand to gently caress one of her excited nipples. "And you're pretty damn bold for a virgin."

Their breathing became ragged and loud. She raised her chin and said huskily, "Just because I've never done it, doesn't mean I don't know what I want."

He teased her nipples to a sensitivity level that made speech nearly impossible. "And what is that?"

Chelle closed her eyes, succumbing to the waves of pleasure that rippled through her. His fingers were magic. "You, Mason. I want you."

From what little experience she had, she expected Mason to rush, to take what he claimed to want as badly as she did. She shivered with excitement as he ran his hands over her as if he were a blind man learning every curve of her. "Open your eyes, Chelle. Look at me."

She did, and he pulled her to him, caressing her with a wondrous blend of roughness and expertise, bringing each inch of her skin alive with his touch. When she raised her hands to undo the buttons of his shirt, he took her hands and placed them back at her sides.

"Don't touch me. I don't want to rush."

She stood there, her body humming beneath his caresses. "What am I supposed to do?" she whispered.

"Enjoy," he growled.

Oh yes.

He began to kiss every place his hands had explored. His lips brushed over her skin. His tongue teased spots she hadn't known were sensitive. "Tell me what you like."

She gasped as his mouth closed over one of her nipples and his tongue flicked back and forth over it. "I like it all."

He chuckled against her breast and ran a hand down her stomach. His fingers parted her folds and exposed her clit. He teased her with his thumb at the same time as his tongue continued its intimate assault, and she dug a hand into his hair. "Oh, that's good, too. You are amazing."

He kissed his way to her other breast, and her hips rocked with pleasure against his hand. He chuckled again. "I've barely started."

His fingers slid back and forth between her wet folds, returning to caress her nub in a way that made her forget she was standing. She was floating before him, aware of nothing beyond his scent, his mouth, and the way his hands played her as if he were tuning a precious instrument.

When he kissed her again, she had already given herself over to his pleasure and her own. She opened her mouth wider to his, placed a foot on the edge of the bed to open herself more to his hand. She couldn't stop herself—her hands went to the enormous bulge in the front of his pants, and she caressed him, loving the hard promise of what he was offering.

He kissed his way down her stomach and across the inner thigh of the leg she'd poised on the bed. "Lie down," he ordered.

She dropped to the bed with an eagerness that sent her backward in a bounce. Desperate to not lose the mood, she scooted forward too far, and ended up half sitting on the floor before him. She was struggling to regain her balance when he lifted her and placed her back on the bed.

"Stay," he ordered with a grin that was sex and humor combined.

Her feet and behind were hanging precariously off the edge of the bed, but she wasn't going anywhere. He dropped to his knees, settled himself between her legs, and balanced her with his hands. His lips moved closer and closer until his hot breath teased her mound. "You're so beautiful."

Chelle gripped the bed sheets around her. With any other man, she would have felt awkwardly exposed, but Mason had a way of looking at her that made her feel as beautiful as he said she was. She was trying to summon enough coherence to say something to him, when his mouth closed over her sex and his tongue began an intimate dance with her clit.

Nothing else mattered. There was only Mason and the fire he sent shooting through her womb. It wasn't just that Mason was good; it was also that he seemed to instantly home in on what brought her the most pleasure. Each time she thought it couldn't get better, he brought her to a new level, changing something he was doing just enough to have her crying out uncontrollably. She'd experienced orgasms before, but her own hand had never brought her to a state of mindless begging.

He dipped his tongue inside her and then laved her sex roughly. She nearly came then, but it was a few moments later, when he slid one finger inside her while his mouth continued to work its magic on her clit, that she had her first mind-boggling, profanity-inspiring climax.

He stood, still dressed and looking as pleased as a pirate surveying his bounty as she tried to gather her thoughts. "Undress me," he commanded.

She raised a hand weakly. "I may need a moment."

"Now," he ordered, and desire shot through Chelle again. She was on her knees almost instantly, and he helped her back onto her feet. He rewarded her obedience with a kiss so hot it almost had her flopping back onto the bed. He tasted of her and him, and the mixture was intoxicating in a way she'd never imagined.

Her hands shook as she pulled his dress shirt out of his trousers and began to unbutton it. Once it was open, she could fully understand why he'd taken his time with her. She ran her hands over his wide, muscular chest. She took her time savoring the hard muscles of his biceps and the flat perfection of his taut stomach.

Licking her lips, she unbuckled his belt and trousers. She slid both his pants and his boxer briefs down, bending to hold them as he stepped out of them. The action freed his erection, and it was now directly in front of her face. She'd seen photos of naked men before, but she doubted there was a more perfect penis in all the world. Like the rest of him, it was beautifully sculpted. The size was a little intimidating. She didn't expect pain her first time, but he was endowed with more than most, at least if magazine surveys were anything to go by.

It seemed a shame to be so close and not taste him. She flicked her tongue across the tip, and he groaned audibly. She looked up at him quickly, then followed her instincts. She took him into her mouth as deeply as she could and caressed him with her tongue.

He grabbed two fistfuls of her hair and guided her backward until she sat on the edge of the bed. At first, she didn't know what to do, but he didn't seem to care. She ran her hands up and down his thighs and moved her mouth up and down on him.

His hands tightened painfully in her hair, and he withdrew from her. "Stop," he ordered. He crawled onto the bed beside her, pulled her to him, then poised himself above her. He swore, rolled, and reached into the pocket of his pants. When he rolled back, sheathed in a condom, he said, "I'm always very careful, but you almost made me forget to be."

"Sorry?" she said in a cheeky tone.

He kissed her deeply, then raised his head. "You're dangerously addictive, Chelle. What am I going to do with you?"

The sadness she'd glimpsed in him earlier had returned, and she didn't want it to be part of their lovemaking, so she deliberately misinterpreted his question. She pulled his head back down for a kiss. With a wiggle of her hips, she wrapped her legs around his hips, a move that brought his cock full against her parted sex. "I have one suggestion, but I don't want to be too forward."

Humor lit up his eyes and mixed with the desire already burning there. He raised and lowered his hips so the tip of his cock grazed her clit again and again. "Aren't you supposed to be afraid?"

She parted her legs farther. "I'm with you. How could I be?"

He claimed her mouth again with a roughness that felt a bit like a reprimand, but she wasn't sure who he was angry with. He kissed his way down her neck and took his time guiding her body once again to a wild, hot frenzy. When she was writhing beneath him, he carefully slid the tip of his cock into her.

Gently. Slowly. Despite how desperately Chelle wanted him, he took his time. There was tightness, but no pain. He began to move in and out of her slowly, and a whole new sensation rocked through Chelle. She moved with him, meeting his gentle thrusts with her own.

"More," she whispered hotly into his ear. "Harder."

He paused. "Are you sure?"

She nodded, and he thrust himself deeper into her. *Oh God.* It felt so good. Better than anything she'd imagined. "Oh yes," she cried out. "Like that."

He raised himself above her and plunged deeply into her, again and again, harder and faster until she was clawing at him and sobbing from the pleasure of it. Just as she was about to climax, he took one of her nipples between his teeth and tugged at it in a way that sent waves of heat through her. The orgasm paused and heightened. Slight pain, intense pleasure. The feelings built upon each other until she was begging him to take her other breast into his mouth. All the while he pounded into her, filling her so completely she thought she'd never feel whole without him again.

When she finally did come, she threw her head back, arching against him, and gave herself completely over to it. She collapsed beneath him. "Holy shit," she said as she tried to catch her breath.

He rolled onto his side, disposed of his condom, cleaned himself off, and then pulled her into his arms. "Glad you enjoyed it."

With her head resting on one of his bulging biceps, she absently ran a hand over his bare chest. "Oh yes. I can only assume you came, too, because I was outside of my body for a few minutes there." She closed her eyes and savored how her body was still humming with pleasure. "Is it always like that for you?" she asked without thinking.

He tensed beside her, and her eyes flew open. He rubbed a hand over his face as if some thought were causing him actual pain. The openness was gone, and Mason was suddenly as distant as a stranger. He moved off the bed and pulled on his trousers. "I'm sorry, Chelle."

Okay. Don't panic. You knew he wasn't staying. Of course, a woman could hope a man would want to linger a bit, but . . .

"For what?"

He frowned at her while he continued to pull on his clothing. "I have to get out of here. I don't spend the night. Ever."

She wrapped the hotel sheet around herself and fought back the tears that threatened to spill over. *This is who he said he was.* Still, it hurt Chelle that he had withdrawn so completely. Okay, so maybe he wasn't the type to stay and cuddle, but couldn't they at least talk? Why did he look as angry as she felt hurt? "I didn't expect you to stay."

He picked his tie off the floor and stuffed it into his pocket. His expression darkened. "I don't believe in relationships or monogamy."

The hurt of a moment ago quickly dissolved. His eyes raked over her with a hunger that made her want him again. It was then she realized he wasn't upset with her—he was angry with himself. "Then leave," she said, pushing him to see the truth.

"I should." He ground the words out, but didn't move. "The problem is I don't want to," he said harshly, looking as if he hated himself for making the admission.

"Then stay," she suggested softly.

He stood there for a long moment, seeming to debate his next move. Finally, he pulled off his shirt and threw it back on the floor. "You leave tomorrow." He shed the rest of his clothing and slid back into bed with her. He pulled her back into his arms, tucking her firmly against his side. She could hear his heart beating loudly in his chest. "This doesn't change anything."

Despite his declaration, Chelle relaxed. Her first time should have left her feeling vulnerable, but oddly it was Mason who it had shaken. Part of her was just as afraid as he was, but at the same time she knew he was letting her see a side of himself he hid from others. This wasn't the smiling, confident Mason who charmed crowds with ease. This was the broken man inside him.

Chelle wrapped her arms around him in an entirely different way than she had earlier and gave him a full-body hug. "You're a better man than you think, Mason."

"You don't know me," he said and turned off the light beside the bed. Still, the way he held her to his chest through the night made her believe that maybe, just maybe, she did.

She was much less sure the next morning, when she woke alone.

Mason wasn't feeling his best the next day as he sat at his desk and answered the landslide of e-mails he'd received. His supposed engagement to Chelle had made it into the national news circuit, and the story had gone viral in a way he hadn't expected it to.

I probably shouldn't have mentioned that Chelle knows the Takedown Cowgirl.

I fucked up royally.

His office phone buzzed. He answered, and Millie said, "You have a call on line one."

"I told you to hold my calls until lunch," Mason snapped. He knew he was taking his sour mood out on the wrong person, but he was too angry to care.

"It's Charles Dery. He told me to warn you if you don't take his call, he'll fly here, and that won't go well for you." Millie repeated Charles's threat in a professional, nondramatic tone.

"Put him through," Mason said tiredly and hit speakerphone.

Charles didn't waste time on the formalities of a greeting. "Didn't I ask you to stay away from Chelle?"

Mason closed his eyes and rubbed his throbbing temples. "You did."

"You had to have her go out there to see you. That's so classically you; I can't be angry about that. But for God's sake, you couldn't keep it out of the news? You had to parade her around and make a big deal about an engagement we both know is fake? Where is your fucking brain?"

If Charles was looking for a fight, Mason wasn't engaging. He completely agreed with Charles on this one. He'd spent hours since he left Chelle chastising himself for sleeping with her and making their little game public. He felt like a complete ass. It was worse, though, than even Charles knew. Mason opened his eyes and slammed a fist down on his desk. "I like her."

"Shit. You slept with her, didn't you? You couldn't keep your dick in your pants, could you?"

Feeling both guilty and cornered, Mason snapped, "How high and mighty you sound when you judge me, but I don't remember you keeping Melanie out of the spotlight. Oh, but wait, that was different, because it was you. You can fool everyone else, but I've known you too long. You don't give a shit about Chelle. You're pissed that someone in that little town you pretend to love might be upset with you. Did you hand your balls to Melanie along with a diamond ring? Because it sure sounds that way to me."

Charles inhaled loudly. He swore a few times, then sighed. "I'm happy for the first time in my life, Mason. You're right—I don't want to lose Melanie or the man I am when I'm with her."

If there were an award ceremony for biggest ass of the year, Mason was certain he would be a shoo-in for winner this year. He ran a hand through his hair. "I don't want you to lose that, either."

"News of your engagement has hit Fort Mavis. They think you came to town and swept Chelle off her feet. No one here has the slightest idea this is a joke. And you're wrong; I do care about Chelle. She's been a good friend to Melanie. I don't want to see her get hurt in this. You might think you like her, but you'll like someone else tomorrow. And another woman by Wednesday. Even if you slept with Chelle, you have to find a way to make sure she doesn't get hurt in this."

"What do you want me to do, Charles?"

"You're the one who is always telling me to put a good spin on things. Spin this into something positive."

"It's not going to be easy. She's leaving today on some big search for who she is. I guess I could say we broke up."

"Have her do it."

Mason grimaced at the phone. "She's probably not talking to me."

"Did you sneak out in the middle of the night?"

Mason didn't bother to lie. This was Charles. "Technically, I waited until morning."

"Mason." Charles said his name as a reprimand.

"I'm aware I'm an asshole." He tapped his thumb on the desk in front of him. "The worst part? I wanted to stay. She has this way of looking at me that makes me forget how completely wrong I am for her. I mean, can you imagine me in a relationship with a woman like that?"

Charles didn't answer at first. When he did, it hit Mason like a kidney punch. "No, I can't." The comment was doubly painful to hear because Mason knew Charles was being honest. "But you do need to talk to her again, Mason. You two need a plan for how to ride out this story in a way that makes it drop out of public interest and leaves her okay to come home."

Home. Could Charles really feel that way about Fort Mavis? Did Chelle?

"I'll call her, Charles. Right after we hang up."

"Mason," Charles said slowly, "you asked for my opinion." He didn't say more. Really, what could he add? It was clear what he thought.

Mason hung up. On impulse, he asked Millie to come in. She took the seat in front of his desk with her tablet in hand.

When he didn't speak at first, she prompted, "You wanted to speak to me?"

Mason stood and walked around to the front of his desk. He dropped into the chair beside her. Her eyebrows rose; that was the only tell that he'd surprised her. "I have a problem."

"Just one?" Millie asked blandly, laying her stylus down on her tablet. A hint of humor lit up her eyes.

Mason sat back and reminded himself that Millie had never given him a reason not to trust her. She was impeccably, consistently reliable. "My engagement isn't a real one. It wasn't supposed to do more than cool down a certain young lady and convince Senator Goss he could vote for my bill because I'm not going to sleep with his wife."

Millie's expression remained impartial. "The engagement looked real enough in the clips I saw on the news."

"That's part of the problem," Mason admitted grumpily.

As if she were asking what he'd like to order for lunch, Millie inquired, "And the rest is?"

"Chelle isn't the type of woman I usually socialize with. I need to put a good spin on this so she can go home with her head held high."

"Senator Thorne, I'm not sure I understand what you're asking me."

"You're a woman. Would it be better for you to break it off with me publicly? Or for me to break it off with you? What do women prefer?"

Millie folded her hands on her lap and asked calmly, "Are you asking me to answer as your secretary, or would you like to hear what I really think?"

Mason sat straighter. "Is there a significant difference in the two?"

"Absolutely."

"Interesting. Start with what my secretary would say."

"Your reputation is your political Achilles' heel. It's what is holding you in this office and stopping you from making a serious run for governor. Continuing the charade might benefit your career. However, considering the circumstances surrounding this engagement, I would suggest you put serious consideration into delicately extricating yourself from this association without incurring the wrath of the woman."

Voilà, the reason Millie was indispensable to him. She not only understood her job but had a good grasp of the bigger picture. Still, he couldn't help but ask, "Okay. Now what is your personal opinion?"

"My impression of Ms. Landon is she doesn't care what the people in her town think of her. She cares about how you feel toward her and whatever went on between the two of you." The look she gave him suddenly turned maternal. "If you have any real feelings for this woman, you'd be a fool to let her go. She's genuine and that's hard to find."

Mason blinked twice and replayed what Millie had said, sure he'd somehow misunderstood. She held his gaze coolly. "Thank you, Millie."

Millie collected her tablet and stylus and stood. "You're welcome, Senator Thorne. Should I order lunch for you, or will you be going out?"

Mason stood. "I have somewhere I need to be. Clear my schedule for the rest of the day."

"Of course," Millie said and walked out of his office.

Mason took out his cell phone and called Chelle.

"Hello?" she said cautiously.

"Where are you?" Mason barked.

"At the airport. I bought a ticket to San Francisco. I decided I have to ride a cable car and see the Golden Gate Bridge before I leave California. My plane boards in twenty minutes."

"Cancel your flight."

"Why?" Her voice went from bemused to slightly disappointed. "Oh, is this about the ring? I completely forgot I still had it on. I could leave it with security here at the airport if you want. Or I could mail it to you. Insured, of course."

"I don't care about the damn ring. Have you watched the news?"

"No."

"We're all over it. Your family thinks we're actually engaged."

"Oh." She made a pained sound. "That's why they've been trying to contact me. I figured I would call them when I landed."

"I'll pick you up at the airport in forty minutes."

She hedged. "I won't be here. My luggage is on the plane. I have to go."

"Do not leave, Chelle."

He could hear her breathing change and knew her temper was rising. He imagined kissing her anger right out of her. That thought brought back a flood of memories of the night before. How she'd felt beneath him, around him, welcoming him into her.

Focus.

"Mason, I don't mean to be harsh, but I don't like you much today."

He lowered his voice. "We need to talk about last night."

"No, we don't. I knew what I was doing, and you never led me to believe it meant anything to you. Waking up alone wasn't a shock. So no, I don't see what we have left to say."

Mason walked as he spoke, heading toward his car. "I shouldn't have left the way I did." His phone switched to Bluetooth as he started the car and peeled out of the parking lot.

Sounding frustrated, Chelle asked, "What do you want from me, Mason? If you're looking for me to tell you I'm okay with what you did, it's not going to happen. That was pretty shitty. I don't care how well we do or don't know each other. You didn't have to end it that way."

Mason ground the gears of his car and merged recklessly into traffic on the highway. "You're right, but don't get on that plane."

With a strangled sound, Chelle asked, "How do you know my parents know? Did you talk to anyone from Fort Mavis?"

The conversation wasn't going as he'd expected. "Charles."

In a horrified tone, she asked, "Oh my God, does he know about us? Are you calling me because he told you to?"

Mason didn't want to lie, but nor did he want to confirm.

Chelle's voice rose. "I am not a violent person. I'm not even an angry person by nature, but if you were here, I would probably hit you again. And this time, I'm not sure I'd feel bad about it. I'm okay with last night, Mason. You know what? It was even wonderful. You were wonderful, okay? But everything else around that, this whole conversation—I don't know what to do with it. Don't come to the airport, because I'm getting on my flight. In fact, I'm boarding now. Good-bye, Mason."

"Chelle—" Mason stopped when he realized she'd hung up.

Shit.

Chapter Nine

"Are you from California?" the man in the seat next to Chelle asked. He was a middle-aged nonthreatening type in a suit.

"No," Chelle answered and sank deeper into her window seat with a sigh. "Just visiting."

"Did you enjoy your stay?"

Some of it, Chelle thought and fought back the X-rated memories of the night before. "It was different than I expected."

The man gripped the armrest beside him as the plane taxied for takeoff. "I hate flying, but I have to for my job. I find that talking to the person next to me makes it easier. Tell me if you'd rather not."

Chelle rubbed her hands over her face. "I'm in a funky mood. It's probably better if we don't. I'd end up talking your ear off."

The man peered around her and out the window. He went a little white as the plane left the ground. His eyes sought hers desperately. "Honestly, you'd be doing me a favor. I usually take a Valium, but I used my last one getting here and didn't realize it until this morning. I don't know you. You don't know me. You can tell me anything. It'll be better than sitting here pretending I'm not about to throw up my breakfast."

The man had a point. They hadn't exchanged names. What harm was there in voicing the thoughts spinning through her head? "If you're sure?"

The man nodded and wiped a napkin across his sweaty forehead.

"So it all started when I went to a wedding a few weeks ago, and I realized I didn't still want to be a virgin when I turned twenty-six . . ." The story poured out of Chelle. She paused briefly when the stewardess delivered their water and a bag of pretzels, then continued her tale. She shared everything, even how ridiculous she'd felt when she'd realized her father might have witnessed her giving a condom back to David. She skimmed over the night she spent with Mason, but didn't leave it out. It was necessary to tell him if he was going to understand why she was upset that she'd actually believed Mason would be there when she woke. "Then right before we got on the plane, he called and told me he wanted to talk. What do you think he wanted to say? Because I figured it couldn't be anything good, so I didn't want to hear it. But what if it was? You're a man. What do you think?"

The man blinked several times, and Chelle pulled herself out of her wild recounting to study his expression. He looked shell-shocked in a pink, flustered sort of way. "My wife wouldn't like me talking about this."

"Oh," Chelle said. "You said you didn't care what we discussed. It was too personal, wasn't it? I'm sorry. I'm so used to everyone knowing more about me than I could ever tell them. There really are no secrets in a small town." She ended her explanation lamely.

He loosened his tie as if it were choking him. His mouth opened and shut several times like a fish gasping for air. The pilot announced their approach to San Francisco International Airport.

The two of them sat in awkward silence as the plane landed. Chelle glanced at him, and he didn't look upset about the landing. She gave his arm a pat and said, "At least I distracted you."

The man pulled his arm away quickly, and it was only then that she noticed a slight bulge in the front of his pants. Chelle turned bright red and spun to face the window. *I may have shared too many details.*

As soon as he could, the man bolted from her side and off the plane. Chelle stayed behind, letting the other passengers follow him, torn between being mortified and laughing. The more she thought about what she'd told the man, the more amusement won.

How was your trip, Chelle? she imagined Sarah asking her.

What would she say? *On the positive side, I am happily no longer burdened with virginity. Yay for me. I also discovered I have a healthy sex drive and the ability to orgasm multiple times. On the negative, I made a fool of myself over a man who gave me every opportunity not to, then accidentally gave a pornographic retelling of the event to a complete stranger, who I believe is running to the nearest church to confess that he liked hearing it.*

Overall, I'd call it a success. She bit her lower lip. *I feel good. Free.* She remembered the way she'd felt for Mason when she'd woken up that morning, before she'd realized she was alone, and amended her inner declaration. *Mostly good.*

And now I'm in San Francisco. She gathered up her bag and exited the plane. *The answer to all of my questions could be here. What am I supposed to be doing that I'm not? Is there something here I can't find back in Fort Mavis?*

Chelle took a spot near the luggage carousel and accidentally met the eyes of the man she'd spoken to on the plane. She was tempted to walk over and apologize again but decided that would probably make the situation more awkward.

"It wasn't easy to get here before you."

Chelle spun around and found Mason standing behind her. She opened her mouth to say something, but he cut her off by hauling her to him and kissing her until she forgot why she was upset with him. When he raised his head, she stood weakly in his arms. "What are you doing here, Mason?"

"I told you—we have to talk." He murmured the words against her neck.

Chelle found it difficult to breathe as images of the two of them, intimately entwined, rushed back. "Talk?"

He chuckled against her ear. "Among other things. All I thought about on the plane ride here was how much I want you. I want to take you in the shower, lick water off those beautiful tits of yours, and fuck you again and again. How far is your hotel?"

"Uh . . ." Chelle couldn't remember. All she knew was Mason had come for her, and she felt deliciously pleased about seeing him again. Yes, waking up alone had been awful, but the sex before that had been too good to not want to have it again. *And I can't get this back home.*

She looked away, seeking guidance, and caught the man she'd flown over with watching them. His eyes were practically bulging out of his head. Chelle nodded toward Mason and raised one shoulder in question. *Should I?*

He went a bit red in the face, but he nodded and gave her a thumbs-up.

Chelle turned back to Mason and handed another day over to what she hoped would be another heavenly experience. "I don't remember, and I don't care." She laughed and threw her arms around his neck. "Take me somewhere amazing."

He made a pleased sound and said, "I intend to." With a hand on her lower back, he started guiding her out of the area.

Chelle paused. "My luggage."

"We'll have someone retrieve it."

As they walked out of the airport and into the sunshine, Chelle turned to Mason. "Are you going to leave again while I'm asleep?"

"No."

"Is that what you want to talk about?"

Mason turned her and pressed her up against the side of a car. Evidence of his arousal was huge and hard against her, bringing a flush of anticipation to her cheeks. "We do need to talk, but I have something else in mind first."

He kissed her deeply, and passion swept through Chelle. How she'd felt that morning was nothing in the face of her need for him now. She arched herself against him and ran her fingers through his hair. "I was so angry with you, Mason, but I can't say no to you. How do you do that?"

Her comment didn't appear to please him. He opened the car door and helped her in, saying curtly, "Some call it a gift."

A gift? Mason wasn't humble when it came to his bedroom skills. Chelle smiled a little at the thought. He was talented, however. Even though Chelle was still incredibly turned on, a part of her felt guilty about it. He could be a tough man to read. He'd said he wanted her. She'd agreed to be with him. Why did he still look as though something were tearing away at his insides? Had he expected her to turn him down?

As they drove along, Chelle reached out and took one of his hands in hers. "What's wrong, Mason?"

He turned a smile on her that was designed to charm her, then looked back at the road. She wasn't fooled. He was as confused as she was. She'd bet her last dollar on that.

He said, "This is wrong, Chelle. The biggest favor I could do for you would be to stay away, but I can't. I want to spend the rest of the day tasting every inch of your body. Charles was angry that we put our fake engagement out for the press to run with. I told him it was a mistake, but I know the media too well to not understand what would happen. On some level, I wanted to publicly lay claim to you. I don't believe in relationships, Chelle, but I don't want another man to be with you—ever. You're mine."

Chelle squeezed his hand. His words did crazy things to her heart. He wasn't saying he loved her. He wasn't vowing to be exclusively hers. What he was describing was carnal and primitively possessive.

When he looked at her, need for her darkened his eyes, and a tingly heat seared through her. It brought out a bold side of her she hadn't known existed. She slid a hand down the front of her pants and beneath her panties. She was wet and excited. He glanced down, then back at the road and said huskily, "Do you want us to crash?"

She settled a finger on her clit and began to tease it in the same manner he had the night before. "I have faith in your ability to drive. How far is it to where we're going?" She loved the flush on his cheeks.

"I booked a suite at a place in Ghirardelli Square."

Mason and chocolate? California sounded like heaven on earth. Chelle continued to caress herself and answered huskily, "Sounds perfect."

"I've never been there, but I hear it's beautiful."

Chelle tipped her head back as the pleasure of her own touch began to heighten. "Even better."

"It's about twenty minutes from here."

"That should be long enough," Chelle said. With slowly increasing speed, Chelle caressed herself until she was breathing heavily and nearing climax. She withdrew her hand and ran a wet finger across his bottom lip.

He grabbed her hand and held it as he licked her juices off her. "God, you taste so fucking amazing. How could someone as innocent as you know exactly what to do?"

Between ragged breaths, she answered, "I read a lot."

His chuckle barely registered.

She undid the front of her pants and guided his hand to her sex. His fingers were a thousand times more talented than hers. She leaned back and closed her eyes, reveling in the way he knew just how to send her into a mindless, writhing state where all that mattered was the promise of release.

There wasn't much about the drive to Ghirardelli Square that Mason remembered. He was reasonably certain he had checked in with the management of the boutique hotel and declined the offer of a butler to guide them to their unit. Beyond that, every moment and every thought he'd had centered on Chelle and the moans she'd made as she'd come.

If he hadn't been navigating lanes of busy traffic full of tourists, Mason would have pulled over and taken Chelle right there on the side of the road. Hearing her cry out as she'd orgasmed beside him had had him out of his mind with desire for her.

The scenario wasn't unique, but how he felt was. The women he'd been with hadn't been shy. He'd had sex in cars before, moving and parked. More than once, he'd been guilty of DWC (driving while coming)—not a safe practice, but a pleasurable one. The difference was that he normally remained in control even during climax.

Chelle had a way of making him forget about everything around them. He wouldn't dare let her touch him while they were driving, because he was certain they wouldn't survive it. Something about Chelle made mundane things exquisitely, unbelievably fresh and all-consuming.

They'd barely made it inside the hotel suite before they were pulling off each other's clothing. His jacket and tie were the first to hit the floor. They rolled against the wall, kissing each other hotly as they feverishly unbuttoned each other's pants and stepped out of them without breaking contact. She whipped her T-shirt and bra off. He pulled his shirt up and over his head, not taking time to unbutton it.

Sex was how he connected with women. He could enjoy a good fuck and remain emotionally untouched. Chelle's caresses threatened his very sanity. He didn't just want her—he needed her, as desperately as a person gasps a breath after being denied air.

He used the last of his coherent thought to sheathe himself in a condom before lifting her off the floor and settling her wet sex onto his throbbing cock. This wasn't the skillful, controlled lovemaking he prided himself on. He dug one of his hands into her hair, while his other hand helped support her as he pounded her against the wall. He could hear her calling out, but God help him, he didn't think he could have stopped had she begged him to. He was too far gone. Luckily, her cries were those of encouragement and pleasure.

He lost himself in the eager play of her kiss and her tightness around his thrusting cock. As he drove himself deeper and deeper inside her, he thought about how he'd felt when he'd realized Chelle had gotten on the plane. This was not just a fucking; it was a claiming. She was his.

Chelle cried out as she orgasmed and dug her nails into his back, clinging to him. He came with a shudder that rocked right through him.

They stood there, with him still inside her, sweaty and panting. He cursed himself for not going slower, for not being gentler with her when she might still be sore from her first time. He buried his face in her neck and said, "Chelle—"

She wrapped her legs tighter around his waist and dug her hands into his shoulders. "Wow."

He raised his head. "I'll take it slower next time. I'm not normally like this."

She smiled up at him and flexed her inner muscles around him. "That's a shame, because . . . holy shit, that was good."

The sated expression on her face was enough to convince him she meant it. He let out a pleased chuckle and lowered her gently to her feet, quickly disposing of his condom before swinging her up into his arms and carrying her toward the bedroom.

With a light laugh, she said, "There's more?"

"You have no idea." He threw a few condom packets on one pillow and laid her gently down across the king-size bed, stretching out on his side beside her. Her hair was fanned out across the sheets and her body was perfection, but what moved him the most was the absolute trust in her eyes as she looked up at him.

In all his life, he doubted anyone had ever looked at him that way, and it confused him. He knew what they had could only be temporary. Yes, what he felt for her was more intense than what he'd felt for any other woman, but that was proof it wasn't sustainable. Like a perfect day or the perfect sunset, nothing that beautiful was meant to last.

That jaded thought didn't diminish how he felt right then. She belonged with him, to him. For that day, that week, or however long it took their wild passion to burn out—he wanted her by his side, in his bed, looking at him just the way she was. He ran the back of his hand softly across one side of her collarbone, briefly over her beautiful breasts, and down to rest on her stomach.

"What are you thinking?" she asked.

He brought his hand up to tuck a curl behind one of her ears. "You're coming back to Sacramento with me."

"I am?" Her eyebrows shot up.

He lazily ran his hand down her other side, pausing to circle one of her puckered nipples. "Yes. I have to be there for meetings, but I can schedule trips. Tell me where you want to go, and I'll take you there."

A little line creased her forehead. "I'm confused, Mason. What are you saying?"

He ran his hand lower, slid a finger between her still-wet folds, and sought her clit. He knew how to tease and retreat, how to circle and then caress her nub. Between lingering kisses across her chest and down her stomach, he said, "You're addictive, Chelle Landon. The more I have you, the more I want you. The thought of you with another man is driving me insane. I want you in my bed tonight. And tomorrow."

Her breathing was already coming faster and harder. He slid a finger inside her and began to pump slowly in and out while moving back and forth over her clit with his thumb. He took one of her nipples between his teeth and gave it a gentle tug. She pushed herself up onto her elbows and said breathlessly, "And after that?"

He pushed her back down and switched his position so he was above her. He slid another condom on and moved his cock back and forth slowly between her lower lips. He took both of her hands and brought them together so he could hold them in one of his above her head. "Don't think. Let yourself enjoy." He dipped the tip of his cock inside her, then withdrew it and used it to tease her intimately until her eyes were wild with need for him to plunge inside her. She arched upward, offering her other breast to his mouth. "Oh yes."

Between deep kisses, he explored her with his mouth, loving how uninhibited she was with him. Even after he released her hands, she remained in that position, gripping the pillow above her head. He enjoyed discovering exactly which touches reduced her to mindless whimpering. There wasn't an inch his hands or his mouth hadn't explored by the time she was begging for him to take her.

He finally slid his cock slowly inside her and watched her eyes widen as he filled her. Her hands came down to his shoulders, and she opened her legs wider beneath him to allow him better access. "Mine."

He pounded into her. She drove her tongue into his mouth for another mind-blowing kiss. The feel of her around him, fucking him with her tongue as well as her sex, demolished the last of his ability to think coherently. It was once again a primal mating he'd lost control over.

They rolled on the bed, and she was above him, raising and lowering herself onto him. Her beautiful, perky breasts bounced up and down. She was wild, and he met her thrust for thrust and dug his hands into her hips to steady her. She cried out his name when she climaxed, and he joined her with a powerful thrust.

She collapsed on him, her body slick against his. He wrapped his arms around her and rolled them both onto their sides, then disposed of his condom and dropped onto his back, pulling her with him. They lay comfortably in each other's arms as they each slowly came back to earth.

In the quiet of the hotel room, a cell phone rang, intruding gratingly. Chelle shifted on the bed beside him, preparing to get up. He held her against him. "You can talk to whoever that is later."

She shook her head regretfully and pushed at his arm. "I know the ring. It's my parents."

He held her tighter and murmured, "Then you should definitely wait until later."

Her phone stopped ringing. She rolled on her side to face him, running her hand over his shoulder and down his arm. "I should have called them this morning. I don't want them to worry."

Their eyes met and held for a long moment, and Mason found it hard to breathe. She was every bit as good and kind as she appeared to be, and that realization terrified him. He felt like a charging bull asked to stop and hold a delicate glass figurine. Could he be with her and not completely destroy her? He hated that he had to ask himself that question and that the answer wasn't a simple *yes*. He kissed her forehead and released her. "Go."

She wrapped a sheet around herself and stood beside the bed. "You said they know about us being engaged?"

Mason nodded, not bothering to cover his own nudity. Her eyes slid down his torso to his cock, which twitched and began to swell beneath her attention. Her blush was about the sexiest thing he'd ever seen.

She blinked several times, then brought her eyes back to his. "What else should I say—about us, I mean?"

Mason rolled to his feet and closed the distance between them. He caressed her upper arms while asking, "What do you want to tell them?"

"The truth. I feel like I already disappointed them by not being honest about where I was going."

"And what is the truth?" Mason asked slowly. He wasn't sure anymore.

Chelle shrugged one of her beautiful bare shoulders, revealing the swell of one of her small breasts. "That this was a joke that got out of hand. That I was trying to help you and didn't realize anyone in the media would care."

He continued to stroke her upper arms. "We both knew what we were doing. When the press asked about us, you weren't shy about claiming you loved me. Why do you think you did that?"

Chelle looked away before answering. "It was fun to pretend our engagement is real."

He pulled her closer, against his arousal. "Some of it is very, very real."

She met his eyes with a smile. "Yes, but not the parts I can tell my parents."

He chuckled. "No, I wouldn't suggest that. But what if we stopped pretending? What if we actually were engaged? You could stay with me in Sacramento, and no one would judge you for it."

Her eyes widened. "Are you asking me to marry you?"

"God, no," he blurted.

She pulled herself abruptly out of his arms. Her chest heaved with emotion. "You . . . you . . ." She stopped and wrapped the sheet more tightly around herself. "I'm going to need a minute alone, Mason."

He took a step after her. "It's the perfect solution."

She raised a hand to halt him. "You make me so angry."

He frowned as a thought occurred to him. "You don't want to actually be engaged, do you? We hardly know each other."

She covered her face with one hand. "Please stop talking."

He took her hand in his and lowered it from her face. "Chelle, you don't want to marry a man like me. The sad realization people come to after they make their vows is that love doesn't change anyone. I'm a man who goes after what I want, when I want, and I don't make apologies for that. If you want to be with me, it's on those terms. But I'll tell you I don't let women sleep over, and I'm asking you to stay at my apartment. If that's enough for you, tell your parents we're engaged, and come back to Sacramento with me."

"For how long?" she asked.

He wanted to say what she wanted to hear, but he couldn't. He could lie to other women, but he couldn't lie to her. "A week. A month. However long it's good between us. When things start to sour, I'll make sure the breakup looks like it's my fault."

The flash of sadness in her eyes twisted his gut. "A month. Wow. Sure you're not being overly optimistic?"

"I've told you before, I don't do—"

She raised a hand to his lips to silence him. "I know." She searched his face. "So if I say yes, we're essentially engaged, if one can be engaged with no intention of getting married?"

He kissed the tips of her fingers and murmured, "Yes."

"And no one will ever know differently?"

"Not from me."

Chelle lowered her hand and looked down at the ring, still shiny on her left hand. "I'll do it on one condition. Regardless of how fake our engagement is, you honor it while it lasts."

He raised her chin so she was forced to look him in the eye again. "You're asking me to be faithful to you?"

The strength he saw in her eyes was one of the many reasons he couldn't walk away from her. "I'm not asking. That's my condition. Take it or leave it." Her lips twisted wryly. "I'm sure you can survive a week without other women."

The condition was surprisingly easy to agree to. He was about to seal their deal with a kiss when she put a hand to his chest and stopped him. "One more thing."

He arched an eyebrow and waited, hoping she wouldn't state something he couldn't agree to.

"We're honest with each other even if we think the other person doesn't want to hear what we really feel. No lies. No pretense. Not when it's just you and me."

He laid one hand over hers on his chest. "Agreed."

"Who is Ruby Skye?" Chelle asked, almost under her breath.

Mason remembered the reporters asking about her, and part of him found pleasure in the hint that Chelle might be as possessive of him as he felt toward her. "She's an old friend from my acting days."

"So you've slept with her?"

"Not in a long time. She'll call and ask me to walk the red carpet with her now and then when she needs a date, but it hasn't been more than that in years."

"The press seems to think you two have a rocky romance."

"I care about Ruby because she's part of my past and I understand what she struggles with. That's it. You asked me to be honest, and that's what I'm being. I can't make you believe me. You either do, or you don't."

She searched his face again and let out a soft sigh. "I do."

"And?" he pushed. He needed to hear her say it.

She let the sheet fall and slid her arms around his neck, bringing herself flush against his chest. His cock swelled against her, and in that moment, he was grateful she hadn't asked him for more, because he was sure he would have agreed to anything. She went up onto her tiptoes, brushing her hard nipples across his chest in a teasing move. "And I want to be with you."

He swung her up into his arms and carried her back to the bed. He joined her and ran an adoring hand over her shoulder, down the curve of her waist, and up to cup her breast. Despite his level of excitement, there was no need to rush. She'd agreed to go back to Sacramento with him.

She was his. The knowledge made each kiss sweeter, each touch more fulfilling.

In the quiet of the suite, Chelle's phone began to ring again, but she didn't make a move to answer it. Between kisses, she whispered, "I'll call them back later."

Chapter Ten

Late the next day, Chelle stretched and arched her back without opening her eyes. She felt completely relaxed and at peace with the world. She smiled when she felt Mason's arm, which had been draped across her, tighten and pull her closer. He murmured her name in his sleep, and any doubt Chelle might have had about her decision to stay melted away.

Mason said he was incapable of love. He claimed he didn't believe in relationships, but what they had was more real than anything she'd ever felt before. Maybe it would only last a week. So what? A month ago she was still in her childhood bedroom at her parents' house, hugging a pillow to her chest and imagining the very thing she was experiencing. If people only allowed themselves to enjoy the things that could never be taken away from them, then their lives would be empty, because no such thing existed.

Growing up as she had, Chelle had been sheltered from some things, but not the harsh realities of life. She thought of the summer her favorite horse had stepped in a hole and broken her leg in several places. The image of her thrashing around on the ground in pain was one Chelle would never forget. She'd only been eleven, but her father had given her the choice of how to put her animal down. They could wait for the veterinarian, which would take hours, or he could shoot her mare and put her out of her misery. At the time, Chelle had been angry with her father for putting the weight of the decision on her, but as she'd grown she'd realized why he'd done it.

He'd wanted her to understand that when you love something, you make a promise to it. Whether it was a horse, a friend, or a grandfather, the promise was the same. Love shouldn't weaken when faced with challenges. In fact, challenges were opportunities for love to show its true strength. It was because of her father that Chelle had been strong enough to stay with her grandfather while he took his last breath and to see the beauty in that. Although it had been one of the hardest moments in her life, she was grateful to have been there.

Did Mason know that kind of love? He spoke of learning harsh lessons and of having no family. Besides Charles, and apparently Ruby, Mason didn't talk about his friends. She wondered if he trusted people enough to allow himself to have them. Real friends, that is.

She rolled onto her side and studied Mason's perfect profile. On the outside, he didn't look like a person who needed anyone. And the things that came out of his mouth sometimes were enough to make even a nonviolent woman like her smack him a second time.

"I'm a man who goes after what I want, when I want, and I don't make apologies for that. If you want to be with me, it's on those terms."

What a self-centered ass.

So why agree to pretend to be engaged to him? Chelle tucked a hand under her head and continued to watch him as he slept. *What's the alternative? Ending this now?*

Making love with Mason was a journey as much as leaving Texas had been. It wasn't the same way twice, and each time Chelle learned something new about herself and him. Mason was sometimes demanding, and his passion took Chelle to a frenzied place where she was wild with need for him. Other times, his touch was gentle and slow, with warm kisses exchanged between stories they shared. They slept in each other's arms, woke, and made love all over again.

Since they'd arrived in San Francisco, they'd been wrapped up in each other as only new lovers could be. They'd ordered food to be delivered and showered together rather than break the magic of their connection.

Reality, however, was waiting just outside the door of the suite. The pretense of their engagement kept it at bay a little while longer.

Mason reached for her in his sleep and gathered her to his chest. Wrapped in his arms, Chelle closed her eyes and once again savored the feeling. *I'm falling for a man who says he's incapable of love. A man haunted by a past he won't discuss.*

He'd lost his mother and his career at about the same time. Was that what had closed his heart off? *What is he blaming himself for?*

And why is it, with a list of so many places I want to go, I feel like I'm where I belong?

A light beep from across the room announced Chelle's phone battery was nearly drained. *Oh crap. I never did call my parents.* Reluctantly, she slid out from beneath Mason's arm and padded across the room to hunt through her luggage for her phone charger. While plugging it in, she saw she had several text messages from her mother, along with a couple of voice mails. Rather than read them, she slipped into one of Mason's shirts, stepped into the other room, closed the bedroom door behind her, and called home.

Her mother answered on the first ring. "Chelle, thank God. Where are you?"

Chelle sank into a sofa and tucked her legs beneath her. "San Francisco. I meant to call you as soon as I landed, but"—she looked at the bedroom door and blushed—"I got distracted."

Her mother made a delicate sound of displeasure. "We were worried, Chelle."

Chelle closed her eyes briefly, genuinely regretting how easy it was to forget everything when she was with Mason. "Sorry, Mom. I really am."

Her mother's tone softened. "Well, it's not every day you get engaged, I guess."

A sudden guilt filled Chelle. She hadn't considered until that moment how her parents would feel about her and Mason. *I can't lie to my mother. Not about something this big.* "There's something I need to tell you."

Chelle jumped at the feel of Mason gently moving her hair aside and kissing her neck. With a voice still deep from sleep, he growled softly, "Who are you talking to?"

Before Chelle had a chance to answer, her mother asked loudly enough for them both to hear, "Is that Mason I hear?"

Chelle turned and met Mason's eyes. There was a mischievous twinkle there. The desire to do the right thing was suddenly trumped by a temptation to test how unflappable Mason was. Chelle swatted at him softly and said, "Yes, it is, Mom. Would you like to say hello to him?"

"I would love to," her mother exclaimed.

Mason straightened, and the look of horror on his face was priceless. He mouthed his refusal. "No way."

Chelle nodded, grinning. She held the phone out to him. "Don't be shy."

Mason looked around, grabbed a pair of his pants that were still on the floor, and stepped into them quickly, as if her mother could see him. He was adorably flustered when he finally took the phone and sat down beside Chelle on the couch. "It's a pleasure to speak with you, Mrs. Landon." Mason went pale in response to something her mother said. "I couldn't." Knowing her mother, Bryn, she wasn't accepting his refusal of whatever she'd requested. "That's a beautiful sentiment, but . . ."

Chelle's curiosity was truly piqued when Mason wouldn't meet her eyes. Comprehension was instant when she heard him give in and say, "Mom."

Chelle's eyes nearly popped out of her head. The guilt she'd felt a moment before was forgotten as she watched Mason's reaction to her mother's enthusiastic acceptance of him. She'd expected him to smoothly charm her, but he was surprisingly awkward and unsure of himself. Chelle put an arm around his back and cuddled into his side.

He looked at her with a fleeting unguarded expression of yearning that opened her heart a little more to him. *He wants to be loved just as much as I do and is just as afraid of being hurt. Oh, Mason.*

A moment later, his mask of confidence slipped firmly back into place, and he answered her mother's questions smoothly. His version of the last few days was so convincing, Chelle had to remind herself it wasn't true. When he said he'd never believed in love at first sight until he'd met her at the wedding, Chelle nearly stopped breathing. He told her mother he realized their engagement would appear rushed to everyone else, but he was a man who didn't require time to know what he wanted.

His expression faltered again at something her mother said. "That's very generous of you, but with my schedule I can't imagine how we'd be able to make it back there. Of course. Here she is."

Mason handed the phone back to Chelle.

Her mother continued, "There is no way my little girl is getting engaged without a celebration. I don't care if you have to hog-tie your fiancé, Chelle—your father and I are hosting an engagement party for you."

Chelle's eyes flew to Mason's. No wonder he'd looked uncomfortable. Her mother was charging ahead as if they were really getting married. *And why wouldn't she?*

Mason clearly expected Chelle to talk her mother out of the event. Chelle opened her mouth to do just that, but snapped her teeth together as she thought of something. *If this is just about the sex, then he's right; we shouldn't go home to see my parents.*

But what if it could be more?

No family was perfect, but Chelle had one that was damn near close. Her parents were loving and supportive. Her cousins—and she'd given up counting how many she had—were opinionated and frustrating at times, but would drop everything if they heard someone in the family needed help. She had a feeling she and Mason had very different lives, and she wanted Mason to experience hers before he left her, if that was what he chose to do.

"The next two weeks are crazy, Mom, but we could come home after that."

Mason frowned at her, but Chelle smiled up at him as if she didn't realize he wasn't happy with her decision. He was far too used to things going his way.

"How does Saturday the twenty-fifth sound?"

"That would be perfect."

Her mother called out the news to her father, then asked, "Do you want something fancy? Or what your father and I had for ours? We had a barbeque, invited the whole town, and made it a barn-raising party for Mr. Finley. Mrs. Nicholson needs a new roof before winter. This might be the perfect way to give her one."

"I would love that," Chelle said softly. *That's exactly the Fort Mavis I want Mason to see.*

"Excellent. I'll make all the plans. Give Mason our love. We can't wait to get to know him."

"I will, Mom. And thank you for not being upset that you heard about our engagement in the news first. It just kind of happened that way."

Her mother's laugh was full of forgiveness. "I was young once, Chelle. I'm happy you found someone."

Tentatively, Chelle asked, "How did Dad take it?"

Her mother sighed. "He'll be fine by the twenty-fifth. He just needs time to get used to the idea."

Chelle pictured her father's reaction and laughed nervously. "I'm surprised he didn't fly out here."

"Oh, he would have had I let him, but I told him if he ruins my chance at grandchildren, he'll sleep in the barn for a month. And he knows I mean it."

Grandchildren? Chelle glanced at Mason, who thankfully didn't look as if he could hear her mother. *Mason doesn't think we'll make it two weeks.*

Her mother added, "I know you're in love, but don't let any man steamroll you. When all is said and done, marriage is about respect and compromise, but that doesn't mean you can't make a stand now and then for what's important. Remember that, Chelle. When love is right, it makes you stronger, not weaker."

"Yes, Mom."

"And use birth control. I want grandbabies, but preferably not before you walk down the aisle."

And that's how you know it's time to hang up. "Bye, Mom. I'll call you tomorrow."

Chelle placed the phone on the arm of the couch beside her and folded her arms across her chest. She didn't know Mason well enough to be able to anticipate how he would respond to her doing the exact opposite of what he wanted. Would he yell? Would he turn cold? Had her small act of defiance brought an early end to their time together? She prepared herself for a myriad of responses.

Amused, Mason watched Chelle brace herself for his reaction. From the proud tilt of her chin to the way her folded arms lifted, parting the front of his shirt and revealing more of her chest than she most likely meant to, she was the sexiest woman he'd ever been with, and the most guileless.

No, he didn't want to go to Fort Mavis to meet her family, but when she looked at him that way, there wasn't a request she could make that he would deny. He was wise enough not to let her know that. He forced himself to sound harsh. He took her upper arms in his hands. "You knew I didn't want to go."

She bit her bottom lip and looked up at him from beneath her lashes. "Yes."

God, it was hard to remember why he was even pretending to be bothered. All he wanted to do was kiss those sweet lips and carry her back to bed. "Yet you agreed that we'd attend something two weeks from now."

The air between them sizzled, and their breathing became labored. It was no use pretending they both weren't turned on by the exchange. "I did," she said, a small smile curling her lips.

"Do you know what that means?" he asked, his mouth hovering over hers.

She shook her head, her eyes riveted to his.

He kissed her gently, then lifted her onto his lap, facing him. He slid a hand between her parted thighs and stroked her already wet slit. Her lips parted with a sigh of pleasure he took advantage of. He dug one hand into her hair and held her head while he plundered her mouth so fully it left both of them shaken.

She writhed on his lap, making the pleased sounds he was quickly becoming addicted to. With other women, the marathon of sex they'd had would have taken the edge off his desire for her. He'd never had trouble walking away from a woman, but the more he tasted Chelle, the more he wanted her.

He raised his head and said, "There is no backing out now. You're mine for the next two weeks. I'm going to enjoy every inch of you, every night."

"Every night?" Chelle asked with a playful smile. Her hands slid down his stomach and undid his trousers. "Are you sure you have the stamina to fulfill a promise like that?"

The feel of her hands closing around his freed cock was so intensely pleasurable he closed his eyes briefly. He knew two weeks would never be enough with a woman like Chelle, but he didn't want to consider what that might mean. He forced himself to stay in the moment, to fully enjoy her without addressing the questions building within him.

Chelle was a natural pleaser, even when it came to sex. In the short time they'd been together, she'd learned exactly how to stroke him, cup him, bring him to a place where he forgot everything but her.

He was greedy for her touch. Desperate for her taste. He wanted to know her, own her, be her obsession as much as she was becoming his.

She slid down onto her knees before him and took him deeply into her eager, hot mouth. Her tongue circled and teased, then stroked the side of him. He wrapped her long hair around one of his hands, holding it out of her face, then leaned back and gave himself over to the fire she set ablaze in him.

She bobbed her head up and down, taking him deeper each time. She kept her lips in a wet, tight circle around his shaft. She circled her fingers just below her lips, moving them up and down along with her mouth, deepening his pleasure. Her other hand cupped his balls, working them and the base behind them with a gentle rhythm that had him tightening and near release sooner than he wanted to be.

Their eyes met, and his hand fisted in her hair. He regretted the action as soon as he saw her expression turn doubtful. She raised her head and asked, "Am I doing this right?"

"Fuck yes. Don't stop," he ordered and guided her mouth back to his cock.

Once again, she worked her magic with her tongue and hands, erasing all thought with her gentle touch. He warned her when he was about to climax, and without missing a beat, her hands took over where her mouth had been. He came on her chest and slumped, momentarily spent.

She stood and returned a moment later with a warm cloth. There was something humbling about the way she washed him. He wasn't used to women taking care of him. She left his side again, then returned with a sheet and pulled it over both of them as she snuggled up to him.

The entire encounter confused him. He wasn't the type to climax before a woman. In fact, giving a woman multiple orgasms was something he prided himself on. "Don't worry," he promised, "we're nowhere near done."

Still in his shirt, she cuddled closer and draped an arm across his chest. "I'll hold you to that tonight. For now, this feels so good."

He slid one arm around her and breathed in the scent of her. She rested her head on his shoulder and sighed with contentment. He'd held many women in his life, but always as a lead-in to sex or in a brief embrace afterward. Until Chelle, he would have said having a woman linger after sex made him feel trapped.

The warm feeling that was spreading through him was as unexpected as it was unsettling. The hand he ran through her hair was not a calculated technique designed to turn her on. He enjoyed the feel of her, every part of her. His caress was merely an extension of that realization.

"Tell me something," he commanded in a low voice.

Without lifting her head, she asked, "What do you want to know?"

"Everything," he murmured and kissed her forehead. As she began to describe the family ranch she'd grown up on, he savored the sound of her voice washing over him. No, two weeks would never be enough, but what would be?

Listening to Chelle filled Mason with a sense of peace he wasn't accustomed to. In that calm place, he admitted to himself the reason he was still pretending to be engaged to Chelle. For the first time in his life, he was enjoying something he'd always considered ludicrous—monogamy.

He knew he wasn't the man for Chelle. Even Charles had said as much. She was innocence and sunshine. He was cold and jaded. Staying with her was setting them both on a course to that ugly day when she would realize she needed more than he could ever give her.

She tapped a finger on his chest lightly. "Are you even listening to me?"

He caught her hand in his and kissed it briefly. "Would you forgive me if I told you I was thinking about how beautiful you are?"

She shook her head against his shoulder. "No, because we said we would be honest with each other, and you're scowling at me. If how I look puts that expression on your face, I'm in trouble." She raised her head. "What are you really thinking about?"

How could he explain that he resented her even while he gave in to his desire to be with her? She made him question who he'd become. She brought the past painfully into the present. He didn't consider himself an emotional man, but memories he'd beaten back nipped at his heels again. To be anything to Chelle, he would have to let her in, and that wasn't something he was willing to do.

Nothing good could come from reopening old wounds. He thought back to who he'd been after his mother's death. Rejected by Irene, reeling from the disappointment he'd seen in his father's eyes, Mason had gone on a drug and alcohol binge and had woken up in an alley behind his favorite bar with the blood of another man on his shirt and hands.

Mason could recall only pieces of that night. He remembered leaving the bar and feeling out of control. A stranger had taunted him and unleashed a rage in Mason unlike any he'd known before or since. The only evidence he hadn't killed the man was the lack of a body beside him when he woke.

Ruby had found him, taken him home, and cleaned him up. She never brought that night up, but it lingered between them. They had a lot in common back then. Ruby was making an insane amount of money from one particular movie she'd starred in that had taken the world by storm, and she was handling her fame as badly as he was handling his loss. She was as deep into substance abuse as he was, and they shared that dark habit together, becoming lovers along the way.

Their tumultuous relationship played out in the press. They were two lost, angry souls trying to raise each other up, but ultimately dragging each other down.

Ironically, it was Ruby who pushed him into rehab the first time. She saw the destructiveness of their lifestyle destroying him, even though she couldn't see it hurting her. When released, he succumbed to the temptation of the lifestyle she still led and spiraled even further down, taking her with him. The day she said she loved him was the day he broke it off with her for good. He didn't love her. How could he claim to while enabling her? He put himself in rehab the second time and stayed the hell away from Ruby for a long time afterward.

A better man would have gone back to save her. Mason was under no such illusion about himself. He chose a path he could control. A solitary one where he was all that mattered. Before long, he was in college and turning his life around.

And Ruby? She hid her addiction well enough to maintain an A-list Hollywood status. Years passed, and a sort of friendship replaced the turmoil they had once had. Neither asked the other questions they didn't want to hear the answers to.

Mason never refused to escort her when she asked. He felt he owed her that at least. She was a stunning woman, but he knew the darkness of her core because his was identical. He didn't binge anymore. He didn't lose control, but the rage was still within him. Caged, but very much alive.

He looked into Chelle's concerned eyes. Who would she become as a result of knowing him? Ultimately, he would fail her, just as he had failed his parents and Ruby.

He hoped Chelle didn't make the mistake of falling in love with him.

I should have sent her away before things got to this level.
Instead, I convinced her to pretend to be engaged to me.
I agreed to anything to keep her with me.
How far will I take this before I admit I'm not the man she thinks I am?

"Mason," Chelle said softly. "You're scowling at me again."

Mason forced a smile to his face. "Sorry." And lied again. "I'm thinking about all the work I have piling up for me in Sacramento. Nice as this is, we should head back tonight."

Chelle straightened beside him. "Of course." She turned toward him, her heart in her eyes, and asked, "Are you upset about something?"

He kissed her deeply, then stood and offered a hand to her. "Let's go shower."

She didn't look satisfied with his response, but she took his hand and walked with him toward the bathroom. He turned on the shower, and they stripped and stepped beneath the hot spray together. As carefully as if he were handling delicate china, he ran his lathered hands over her. After rinsing her, he sank to his knees before her and positioned one of her legs on the seat in the corner of the shower. He kissed his way across her thigh and to her parted sex.

When he flicked his tongue across her swollen clit, she gripped his shoulders tightly with both hands. There was so much he couldn't give her, but he could give her this. Again and again, as often as she wanted.

Chapter Eleven

Chelle was on her way back from the ladies' room at the pizza place she and Mason had randomly chosen, when she saw him talking to a curvy brunette. She ducked behind a planter. The woman was obviously flirting with him. She flipped her long hair over her shoulder and arched her back, displaying her enormous, barely restrained breasts.

It was easy to feel threatened by the number of women Mason attracted, but opportunity didn't define a man. She and Mason had spent a magical two weeks together, and she refused to believe it hadn't meant as much to him as it had to her.

Not much happened in Fort Mavis, but with Mason, every day was an adventure. Mason had meetings he needed to attend, but when he was done for the day, he always had a surprise for her. Sometimes it was a local show, or he'd tell her to pack an overnight bag, and they were off to somewhere she'd mentioned she wanted to see.

With his private plane, he'd taken her more places than she would have seen in a month of traveling alone. They'd toured the Grand Canyon, won and lost money in Vegas, and gone skiing in Oregon. Chelle felt like a child playing hooky from her life, but she was enjoying every moment of it. Mason was attentive, funny, and an amazing lover.

Yet every once in a while Chelle wondered if it were too good to be true. This was one of those times. She stood silently behind the large plant and waited to see what he would say to the woman, who was holding out a paper that Chelle would have bet her last dollar had the woman's number on it. *Don't take it, Mason. Please don't take it.*

Mason had that smooth smile on his face that made it impossible to know what he was thinking. A waiter asked Chelle if he could get by and blocked her view for a moment. By the time Chelle looked back, the woman was already walking away.

Crap.

The woman stopped, looked toward where Chelle was hiding, and began walking in her direction. For a split second, Chelle thought she was going to ask her why she was hiding, but the woman glanced past her, evidently in search of the bathroom.

Chelle couldn't help herself. She asked, "Is that Senator Thorne?"

The brunette looked up with a dreamy smile. "It is. I recognized him right away. He's even better-looking in person than he is on TV."

"Did he say anything interesting?" Chelle gave herself an inner smack for asking, but that didn't stop her from hanging on the woman's next words.

The gorgeous brunette wrinkled her small nose. "He said he's off the market. Engaged to some woman from Texas. Why are the good ones always taken?"

Chelle let out a long relieved sigh. "He told you he's engaged? That's awesome."

"Sure," the woman said, "if you're the woman from Texas."

With a smile as big as the state she was from, Chelle said, "I am," and headed back to where Mason was sitting. He stood as soon as he saw her. She threw her arms around his neck and gave him a kiss that rocked him back on his heels. Then, as if nothing had happened, she took her seat and reached for a slice of pizza.

With eyes freshly lit with desire for her, he sat down across from her. "What was that for?"

"I'm happy," she said through her giddiness.

A smile tugged at his lips. "Apparently."

Chelle took a bite of pizza. There was no way she was going to tell him why. Instead, she chewed slowly, then asked, "Are you going to tell me where you're taking me tomorrow? You said we'd stop somewhere on the way to Fort Mavis. Want to give me a hint?"

"No, I like to surprise you." He cocked his head to one side as he spoke. It was a playful move that always made her fall for him just a little bit more. He may have used that expression on other women, but Chelle didn't like to think so.

"And I like that you like to surprise me."

Mason chuckled and folded his arms across his chest. "You're a funny woman, Chelle."

Secure in his attraction to her, Chelle fluttered her eyelashes at him and joked, "By funny you mean the sexiest woman you've ever met."

He laced his fingers through hers on the table between them. "You're definitely that." He turned her hand over and caressed her wrist. "You're also the happiest."

Chelle tried to gauge why his comment didn't sound like a compliment. "Is that a problem?"

His silence wasn't reassuring.

Breathe. Don't assume anything. Let him tell you how he feels.

Finally, he gave her hand a light squeeze. "These past two weeks have flown by. I didn't expect them to."

"Shocked we made it this long?" she joked.

His face remained serious. "Yes."

Chelle took a calming breath. For as much as Mason could be an outrageous flirt, when it came to expressing how he felt, he didn't often phrase it the way he meant it. "Do you know what I'm doing right now?"

A slight frown creased his forehead. "No, what?"

"I'm waiting for you to say something sweet that makes up for your admission that you thought you'd be sick of me by now."

"It wouldn't have been your fault. I have a very low tolerance for substantial time with any woman."

Chelle pulled her hand from his, placed it on her lap, and raised an eyebrow. "Still waiting."

"I could tell you that you're all I think about. How I find myself checking the clock, counting the hours until I get to see you again. But"—he leaned forward, shot her a wolfish smile, and winked at her—"you're fun to rile up."

Chelle threw her napkin at him and laughed. "You're so bad."

"Is that a problem?" He threw her question back at her, his eyes bright with humor.

"No," Chelle said honestly. "I like it."

He held his hand out to her, and she placed hers back in his. "Is there anything you don't like?"

"Sure," Chelle answered, but she had to stretch for something. She may not have figured out the rest of her life yet, but she was on one hell of a fun tangent. "Stray cats make me sad. I want to take them all home with me, even though I know I can't. That's frustrating."

"Cats, huh?"

"Well, anything like that, really. I hate seeing a big problem and feeling like I'm too small to fix it. You must be very proud of what you do, Mason. You make a difference."

Mason's expression turned guarded. "Sometimes."

"Are you kidding? The water bill you're sponsoring will have a huge impact on California."

Mason sighed. "The vote will be close. It's a controversial topic. The opposition is heavily funded. Change costs money, and no one likes that."

"It'll pass. Sometimes you have to trust that things will work out for the best."

He looked at her for a long moment. "I'm not a big fan of trusting anyone or anything."

Ouch.

"That's your choice, Mason. But it's not mine. I prefer not to look for dead fish."

"What?"

Chelle hesitated, but only for a moment. Mason could benefit from Grandpa's wisdom. "My grandfather used to say happiness is a choice. He'd say, 'Take two people to a lake on a perfect day. One of them will be awed by the view and close their eyes to savor the cool breeze. The other one will spend the whole time talking about how every lake has dead fish in it.'"

Mason held up a hand as if he were smoking a joint. "Did your grandfather . . . you know?"

Chelle didn't rise to the bait. "Laugh all you want. He was a wise man who raised a good family, and he died happy, surrounded by people who loved him. You can't argue with a life lived like that."

No, you can't, Mason thought and put down money for the bill. There was a wholesomeness about Chelle that all the sex they'd shared hadn't diminished. She had been, and still was, too good for him.

Mason had always been what some people would call vain. He preferred the term *confident.* He knew what women wanted. They liked money, good looks, and to be physically pampered in and out of bed. He didn't offer them more, and they didn't demand it. He'd been an ass to so many of them, and they'd accepted it. Maybe that was why he didn't enjoy their company for long. He didn't like who he was when he was with them.

Chelle was different. She knew what she wanted, and in her adorably stubborn way, she wouldn't settle for less. "What do you see in me, Chelle?" he asked, not realizing at first that he'd asked the question aloud.

Chelle's eyebrows rose in surprise, then her expression softened, and she gave him a smile so sweet it twisted him all up inside. "I see a man who wants the world to think he has everything but is actually very lonely. You have a wild side, but you don't want that life anymore. I think you're on a journey to discover who you are, just like me, only you're more afraid of change than I am."

Mason frowned. "I'm not afraid of anything."

"No? Tell me one person you love. I bet you can't even say the word."

Mason stood. "It's late, and I have a car picking us up early tomorrow morning."

Chelle walked up to him and laid a hand on his shoulder. She went up on her tiptoes and kissed his lips lightly. "You're a good man, Mason Thorne. That's what I see."

I hope you're right, Chelle. Mason gathered her to him and kissed her soundly. The scent of her, the feel of her lips was all it took for him to crave her so much it hurt. He growled, "You talk too much. Let's go home."

"I like it when you get all bossy."

Mason's mood lightened. A laugh rumbled in his chest, and he felt years younger. He put an arm around her shoulder, and they walked out of the restaurant together. "You like everything."

She tapped a finger on her chin playfully. "Not everything, but I do have a mental list of what I'm curious about."

Mason stopped short and looked down at her. "Really?"

She stretched up and whispered a list of things into his ear that had his cock throbbing with excitement. None of the items she mentioned would have shocked anyone in his crowd, but from her lips, they sounded downright decadent. "It looks like I'll be changing our destination for tomorrow."

She gave him a saucy grin. "Only if you want to."

"Oh, I want to."

Chapter Twelve

Mason didn't give Chelle a single hint about where they would stop on the way to her parents'. They told her family they'd be arriving late in the afternoon, and that was all Chelle knew for sure. A driver came to take them to the airport and a private plane, but not the one they had taken during their other trips. This one was much bigger.

When they boarded the plane, Chelle was curious about the rooms that were off the main cabin. She started walking in the direction of them and said, "Look at this place. I have to see what's back there."

"No," Mason said firmly and turned her back to face the main cabin.

"What don't you want me to see?" she asked, not sure she liked being denied anything so casually.

He guided her to a seat, kissed her lightly, and said, "One of your surprises."

"Good answer." Chelle found it impossible to stop smiling after that.

Over the next few hours, they chatted easily over breakfast. Even though Mason looked as if he were born in the jeans and cowboy boots he'd chosen for the trip, Chelle wanted to make sure he was prepared for what he was about to walk into. She'd spent enough time in his world to know how different it was from hers. "Fort Mavis has layers like an onion. Not all of them are instantly appealing, but they grow on you. If you spend time downtown, you're sure to meet Mountain Man Mike. He walks around, even on hot days, with a long coat and a survival backpack he says he uses when he's in the mountains. No one has ever seen him leave town. We're pretty sure the only mountain he visits is the top of old Farmer Jones's horse shed, but he's harmless. His children moved away but returned to take care of him. They can't get him to move back north with them any more than they can get him to take off his backpack."

"Sounds like quite a character."

"One of many," Chelle said as she thought about the only place she'd known until recently. "I can understand why Mike doesn't want to leave. In Fort Mavis, people take care of their own. He's afraid if he goes to the city, doctors will lock him away somewhere they consider safe. He doesn't hurt anyone, and more times than not, he'll help a person out if he comes across someone in need. People in town watch out for him. They make sure he eats and gets home each night."

"Why do I get the feeling you're leading up to something with this?" Mason leaned back in his seat and crossed one ankle over the other, looking completely at ease.

Not at all how Chelle felt when she imagined Mason in her hometown. "I am, I guess. Fort Mavis is backward in some ways, and the people there aren't known for keeping their opinions to themselves. But if you get past that, it's truly a beautiful place. Most of the families have been there for so long we all feel like family even if we're not related."

"Charles seems to like it well enough. He's moved his business south to spend more time there."

"We love Charles. He's kind of a celebrity to us. When he flies in and his limo pulls through town, people wave like the queen is passing by. It's amusing to watch. Even Mountain Man Mike stops and smiles. He thinks Charles is James Bond, and no one can convince him differently. I think it's those dark glasses Charles wears. Makes him look mysterious."

Mason shook his head and laughed. "Charles probably eats that up."

Chelle chuckled. "He might. I'm sure trying to fit in has been humbling for Charles. You should see him ride a horse." Chelle shook her head in amusement. "Not good. Funny as all hell, but not good."

Their lighthearted conversation carried them through the rest of the flight to Galveston. Upon landing, however, Chelle couldn't take it anymore. She followed Mason into the backseat of the town car he'd hired and said, "Seriously, where are we going?"

He tucked her into his side and put an arm around her shoulders. "You're tense this morning. Usually you like to be surprised."

Chelle gripped his jean-clad thigh. "I am tense. We're going home to meet my parents. I didn't realize I'd get nervous about it, but the more I think about what we're doing, the more ways I see this possibly going wrong. What if they figure out we're not really engaged? They'd never understand." She closed her eyes and rested her head against his arm. "I am not a good liar."

His breath was hot against her ear as he whispered, "You just need to relax and go with it. Luckily for you, I know the perfect way to rid you of all that tension."

Her eyes flew open, and she turned her head toward him. "You do?"

He kissed her gently. "Oh yes. And it looks like we're here."

Chelle sat up. They'd stopped in front of a historic-looking three-story brick building with dark-green wooden trim, sandwiched between two bland office buildings. The large bay windows on the first floor were full of flowers and vases, but there was no sign announcing if it was a florist shop or a private home. "Are we visiting someone?"

He stepped out of the car and offered his hand to her to help her out. "You could say that."

Mason opened the door to the building and held it for her. Chelle hesitated, but not for long. She trusted Mason. Plain and simple. She stepped into a room that looked like an odd mixture of a flower shop and a waiting room. A young woman in a cream dress suit stepped out of the back room to greet them. Her blonde hair was pulled back in a tight professional bun.

"May I help you?" she asked in an English accent.

Mason stepped forward and shook her hand. "I'm here by invitation."

"Number, please." The woman looked down at a computer tablet and waited.

"Five-nine-three-four-T."

The woman used a stylus to mark something on her tablet, then smiled. "Welcome. We hope you enjoy your visit. Follow me, please."

"I'm sure we will," Mason answered calmly and guided Chelle with his hand on her lower back. The woman punched in a code beside a door that led behind the reception area.

Chelle sought Mason's hand with hers. "What is this place, Mason?"

"Patience, Chelle," Mason said with a smile. "You're going to love this."

The room they entered was richly decorated in off-white furniture and wallpaper. Subtle gold accents gave the room a sparkle. Each wall of the room was covered from floor to ceiling with white shelving behind glass doors. Chelle's eyes nearly popped out of her head when she realized what the store sold.

A black woman dressed similarly to the woman who had greeted them stepped forward. Her smile reminded Chelle of the manager of the first hotel Mason had taken her to, though her accent was French. "Welcome. I would introduce myself, but we prefer not to use names here. Is this your first visit?"

Chelle's eyes flew to Mason's.

He didn't hesitate with his answer. "Yes, but I've heard good things about your establishment."

The woman's smile warmed. "Our clientele maintains a high standard of discretion, but it's always a pleasure to have someone of your caliber referred to us. Do you have anything in particular you're looking for?"

Mason nodded in acknowledgment of the compliment, then looked down at Chelle. "My fiancée has a few ideas."

Chelle turned bright red, then looked from Mason to the woman and back. "I do?"

Mason leaned down and kissed her cheek. "You weren't too shy to tell me last night at the restaurant."

Chelle waved a hand at the woman watching them and then at Mason. "That's because it was just you and me. I can't tell her."

The woman's lips pressed together as if she were holding back a smile. "Perhaps you should look around on your own first, yes? I'm here if you have any questions. All of our merchandise is made from the highest quality metals. If it looks gold, it is. The diamonds are very real, so there is no need to ask. No prices are listed. If you must inquire about the cost, you are most likely here by mistake, and we will happily offer you a list of alternative shops."

"Your frankness is appreciated, but not necessary," Mason answered with a casual smile. "I'm sure we'll find several items to fit our needs."

As soon as the woman was out of earshot, Chelle grabbed one of Mason's hands and exclaimed, "Oh my God. First, I didn't know there were so many types of sex toys." Her eyes lingered on one particular shelf while she said, "I can't even figure out what people would do with some of these things." She shook her head and looked back up at Mason. "And second, what kind of place won't tell you how much something costs?" She pointed at a diamond-studded gold toy. "Why would anyone put diamonds on a vibrator?"

Mason nuzzled her neck and growled, "You'd have to try it and tell me."

An image of Mason using the gold vibrator on her, dipping it inside her and slowly pulling it out of her, was enough to wash away all of her embarrassment. Sure, her time with Mason didn't match the fairy tales her mother had read her as a child, but who the heck wanted a glass slipper when they could have something from this store? She pulled him toward the gold vibrator and peered at it through the glass. "What would I do with something that expensive?" Mason chuckled and Chelle quickly added, "I know what I would do with it, but I mean, where would I keep it? In a safe? I can't let you buy me something that expensive."

Wrapping his arms around her from behind, Mason murmured, "Trust me, the last thing I'm thinking about right now is how much anything here costs."

A sudden idea came to her, and she spun in his arms. "Have you bought toys for other women?" She didn't want to imagine it. She knew she was being ridiculous. He'd been with other women. Many, by his own admission.

"I've never considered them necessary, but if you're curious about them, they are."

His answer couldn't have been more perfect. Chelle relaxed. "I'm sorry. Even if you did, it's none of my business. It's not like we're really getting married."

Mason rested his chin on her forehead and sighed. "When it comes to you, Chelle, I can honestly say I have no idea what I'm doing." Chelle stopped breathing, not sure what he meant. He stepped back and lightened the mood by joking. "Except when it comes to toys. I have a pretty good idea what most of these items are for. And I'm confident we could figure the rest of them out."

Chelle looked up at him, and her heart swelled with something that felt frighteningly like love. "Mason, thank you."

He cocked his head to one side and asked, "For what? Bringing you here?"

She hugged him. "For making these last two weeks the most amazing of my life. I was worried what you would think of Fort Mavis. And I was worried about what they would think of you. But none of that matters. You make me happier than I can ever remember being. And maybe this won't last, but I will always be grateful that I had this time with you."

Mason looked away for a moment. He let out an audible breath. "I have failed everyone I've loved."

Chelle hugged him even tighter and whispered, "Then maybe you've loved the wrong people."

The blonde woman cleared her throat beside them. "Did you find something you'd like?"

Chelle nodded her head. "Yes, two weeks ago."

Mason kissed her briefly, then stepped back and said, "We'd like that vibrator, some watermelon lubricant, and . . . do you have a waterproof vibrating glove?"

"We do. Would you like the items sent to you, or will you be taking them with you?"

Mason smiled at Chelle and shrugged. "We still have a two-hour flight."

Chelle doubted toys would be necessary, since she was already dripping wet as she imagined how she and Mason would spend that flight.

Mason was a confident lover, but as he led Chelle back onto the plane he'd rented and into the bedroom with a built-in Jacuzzi tub, he wanted everything to be perfect. From the moment Chelle had whispered her fantasies into his ear, he'd wanted to make them a reality for her.

Although he'd always prided himself on pleasing women, this was different. It felt important somehow.

"Wow." Chelle took in the plane's bedroom. "Now this is how to join the Mile-High Club."

The packages from the store they'd visited in Galveston had already been placed on the bed. He closed the door behind him and said, "Come here."

She pulled her shirt over her head and dropped it on the floor. "You come here."

That brought a smile to his face. "Is that any way to say thank you?"

She unsnapped her bra and let it fall to the floor beside her shirt, proudly displaying the most perfect breasts he'd ever seen. "I don't feel it's appropriate to thank you for gifts until I've decided if I like them or not."

"Really?" he said, unsnapping his jeans and stepping out of his shoes at the same time. "You don't think you'll enjoy them?"

She shed the rest of her clothing and playfully stood there as if she weren't killing him slowly with her teasing. With a shrug, she said, "Diamonds may not be my style."

He pulled his shirt over his head and quickly stepped out of the rest of his clothing. His cock bobbed in the air as he walked toward her. "I thought we'd start with the glove." He walked until he stood less than a foot from her and ordered softly, "Put it on me."

She turned away from him and bent to search through the bags for what he'd requested. He took advantage of her stance. He placed both hands on her hips and ran his cock back and forth between her parted butt cheeks. She froze.

He shifted so he grazed her wet lower lips, and kissed his way up her spine. Skillfully, he dipped the tip of his cock into her sex and moved it back and forth over her clit. She moaned and braced herself against the bed, arching her back with pleasure. "The glove, Chelle."

In slow motion, as if thought was a struggle for her, she opened the box and pulled out the glove. She put it on his hand and straightened, holding on to his forearms. He pressed a button on it, and the room filled with a buzzing sound that wasn't overly romantic.

Chelle laughed. "It sounds like an insect invasion."

He slid his hand down one of her legs. Each of his fingers was now vibrating. He'd never used one before, but he'd heard about them and had no problem coming up with ideas.

He continued to kiss her while he moved his cock back and forth against her slit and experimented with where she enjoyed the glove the most. He circled her nipples, loving how tight and pert they became beneath the vibration. He massaged her back with it before returning his attention to the front of her. All the while he moved intimately against her wetness and kissed every inch of her.

He turned her around and pushed her back on the bed. Her eyes were raging with need for him. He slipped on a condom before joining her, then lay beside her and kissed her passionately and deeply. When he finally brought his gloved hand to her sex, she was already moaning. He placed his vibrating thumb on her clit, working it in light circles, experimenting until she was moving herself against his hand. Then he slid his middle finger deep inside her and sought the spot that many men found elusive on a woman. Finding it was an art, not a science. He knew he'd found it when she started to swear and beg him not to stop.

He pumped one finger in and out of her, slowly at first and then with more speed. He inserted a second finger, and she swore again softly. She was tightening around his fingers, and her preclimax flush was spreading up her gorgeous chest, when he removed his hand and thrust himself deeply inside her. She spread her legs widely for him, and he pounded down again and again until she cried out in release.

Only then did he bring his gloved hand back to her clit. He knew he could make her come again. She kissed him hotly. Her hands clung to him as he thrust into her again and again while using his vibrating fingers to send her soaring toward her second climax.

Her second cry was muffled in their kiss, and he came wildly with her.

He disposed of his condom, removed the glove, gathered her into his arms, and kissed her temple. "So what's the verdict?"

She snuggled against his side. "That may be my favorite toy, but I really should try the other before I say for sure." She kissed his shoulder. "Will we have time before we land?"

A deep laugh rumbled through Mason's chest. "We haven't left the ground yet."

She hugged him and laughed. "Really? Because it felt like we did."

He closed his eyes and admitted to himself that it had been the same for him.

He realized he'd done a piss-poor job of keeping his promise not to lie to her. He'd told her he wasn't afraid of anything, but the truth was what he felt when he was with Chelle scared the shit out of him.

For the first time in his adult life, he was with a woman he couldn't imagine life without, but he didn't know if he was capable of the kind of love that came naturally to her. She wasn't someone who would accept only a part of him. She'd want everything.

Letting her in would mean opening the door to the past.

Chapter Thirteen

The heat of the Texan afternoon went unnoticed as she and Mason walked, hand in hand, down the steps of the plane and onto the tarmac. If her feet touched the earth, she didn't feel it. She was floating, wrapped in a cocoon of bliss. She'd joked she couldn't imagine why anyone would have a Jacuzzi on an airplane. Now she couldn't imagine flying without one.

She and Mason had just had a glorious, thought-erasing couple hours of sex, during which she'd discovered she loved the taste of watermelon and that diamonds felt pretty damn good. Although she'd showered and dressed, she knew she was sporting a goofy post-sex smile. Mason had the same expression, so she didn't bother to try to hide how good she felt. She should have left Fort Mavis a long time ago.

She yawned and chuckled. It was only late afternoon, and she was exhausted. She considered calling her parents and telling them she would see them in the morning. She didn't think, though, they'd appreciate the reason behind her desire to take a nap.

She felt Mason tense beside her and followed his gaze to a limo that pulled up beside the plane. His expression shifted to carefully welcoming as Charles and Melanie stepped out of the limo and walked toward them.

Chelle waved to Melanie and exclaimed, "I didn't know they were coming out to meet us. Isn't that nice?"

Even though Mason was smiling, Chelle could still feel the tension in him. "It might be."

Chelle stepped away from Mason to hug Melanie. Melanie looked her over, then did the same to Mason, and smiled knowingly. "Well, look at the happy couple."

Chelle blushed and hugged Melanie again. She whispered, "You have no idea. I can't talk about it now, but I'm in heaven. Mason is incredible."

Melanie frowned.

Charles asked Mason if he could speak to him for a moment. The two of them walked to the other side of the limo.

Melanie's expression remained concerned, and Chelle was irritated by the negativity she was sensing in her friend. "What?"

"Nothing," Melanie said, but it was obvious she was holding something in.

Chelle put her hands on her hips. "Whatever you're thinking, keep it to yourself. You and Sarah are the ones who encouraged me to have an adventure. Well, I'm having one. And it's better than anything I ever let myself imagine."

Melanie pursed her lips and didn't say anything.

Chelle continued, "I know what you're thinking. Mason isn't the type of man who settles down. You don't want me to get my heart broken. You think I've forgotten that this whole engagement is fake. Well, news flash, I'm not an idiot. I wouldn't be with Mason if he was even looking at other women. He's not. I don't know if what we have is going to last, but it's not fake. Not anymore. Not to me. Not to him."

Melanie opened her mouth to say something, then clamped it shut again.

Chelle threw her hands up in the air and said, "And I realize that bringing him here may not have been the best idea I've ever had, but he needs to see what a real family is like. He's never had one, at least not by my definition. I want him to see that love can work."

Melanie was round-eyed, but she held her silence.

"You think I'm crazy to fall in love with a man like Mason, don't you? That he'll be with another woman by next week. You're wrong."

Melanie raised a hand in protest. "I don't think you're crazy, but I do agree with some of what you said."

"I don't care what you think." Chelle crossed her arms over her chest. "I don't care what anyone thinks. All I know is how I feel when I'm with him. Don't tell me he doesn't feel the same, because I won't believe you."

Melanie put an arm around Chelle and just held her. "I want nothing more than for you to be right, Chelle."

Chelle hugged her back. "I am. I know I am."

The sound of male voices rising in anger made both women turn in the direction of Mason and Charles. Although Chelle couldn't hear what they were saying, it was obviously not a pleasant conversation.

Don't ruin this for me, Charles. Please.

Chelle brought one hand to her lips and watched the two men become more and more upset with each other. "Are they arguing about me?"

Melanie winced as she watched the men. "My guess is yes. Charles asked Mason to stay away from you. I didn't know how serious he was about it until after you left, and we talked. He was furious when he saw the two of you in the news. He was hoping Mason would call off the engagement and not bring the charade here." She looked at Chelle. "Even I don't understand why Mason is taking it this far."

Chelle clasped her hands in front of her. "He wants to be with me. Does it have to be more complicated than that?"

Melanie shook her head. "It's a dangerous game you're playing, Chelle. The whole relationship is backward. Aren't you supposed to date, figure out if you want to be together, and then tell the world you're getting married?"

Without looking away from Mason and Charles, Chelle said, "Oh, right. I've done this all wrong. I should have gone to New York, slept with a man I barely knew, then run back home to hide from him." The sound of Melanie's harshly indrawn breath told Chelle she'd gone too far. She felt instantly contrite. "Sorry, Mel. I didn't mean that. I don't feel like justifying what I have with Mason—that's all. But I shouldn't take it out on you."

Melanie sighed. "No, you're right. What you do with Mason is no one's business but yours. I'm not sure we can convince Charles of that, though."

The two men were still standing toe-to-toe, snarling at each other. Chelle asked, "Do you think one of them will throw a punch?"

Melanie gave Chelle a quick pat on the shoulder. "I don't know, but let's not give them a chance to get that far. We told your parents we'd drive the two of you to their house, and it's probably best not to take a brawl there."

Chelle closed her eyes briefly. "My parents. They do understand that I'm staying with Mason in town, don't they?"

Melanie chuckled. "I wouldn't bet on that."

"Did you see my father today?"

Melanie nodded.

Chelle continued, "I haven't spoken to him since I left. How is he taking it? My mom said he's coming around to the idea."

Melanie rubbed her jaw with her thumb. "You know fathers. They're slow to get used to their little girls growing up."

Shaking her head, Chelle asked, "I know he's only upset because he cares. I don't understand Charles, though. What is he so upset about? He's not even related to me."

They started walking toward their men and Melanie said, "Charles has been Mason's friend for a long time. He knows what he's capable of. He doesn't want to see him hurt you."

While they were still out of earshot, Chelle added, "Can you give Charles a message for me later? A person who has no faith in someone he claims to love is not what I would call a very good friend."

Mason took several calming breaths when he saw Chelle and Melanie approaching. If the visit weren't so important to Chelle, he would have turned his back on Charles and Fort Mavis. He hadn't left the airport yet, and he was already questioning not only his friendship with Charles but his sanity for agreeing to come to that godforsaken town in the first place.

He and Charles had disagreed about things in the past but never like this. He'd always thought that although they were different, they would support each other, no matter what.

The truth was in Charles's eyes when he'd told Mason what a mistake it had been to come back to Fort Mavis. It didn't matter that Charles had chosen his words carefully; Mason had understood exactly what he was saying. Charles didn't want Mason fucking up his perfect little town.

He'd asked Mason to make up an excuse, any excuse, to turn around and leave. And that was the moment Mason had realized how important Chelle had become to him. If being with her ended his friendship with Charles, then so be it. Charles hadn't taken hearing that truth well.

There had been nothing left to do but stand there, glaring at each other. They'd talked their way into what Mason, as a politician, would call a no-win, no-compromise standoff. In his experience, those were best walked away from. Battles like that tended to get bloody and ugly, with nothing achieved as a result.

Mason welcomed Chelle's appearance. He plastered a smile on his face and put an arm around her waist. "Are we ready to go? What time did your parents say dinner would be? Do we have time to freshen up at the hotel first?"

Chelle made a face and said, "My parents want us to stay with them."

Mason looked at Charles and said, "That sounds perfect."

"Really?" Chelle asked in surprise. "They'll probably put me in my old bedroom and you in one of the spare rooms, but I know it will mean a lot to them to have us there."

"I'm fine with whatever," Mason assured Chelle and felt a bit guilty when he saw how happy she was with his answer.

She hugged him. "We'll have to get up early tomorrow morning. Our engagement party is half roof-fixing and half barbeque. Both take time. It'll be a full day, so it might work out to be there."

"I can't wait," Mason said and guided Chelle toward the open door of the limo.

Before Mason had time to join her, Charles blocked him with one arm and asked, "Tell me this isn't a publicity stunt for you. I know being with Chelle has helped you in the polls. Don't use her as part of some political campaign."

Mason bared his teeth at Charles in what was barely a smile. "Get the fuck out of my way, Charles."

Charles dropped his arm, and Mason climbed into the limo beside Chelle. Melanie and Charles sat across from them.

Chelle seemed to sense his mood despite his effort to conceal it from her. She scooted closer to him and put a supportive hand on his thigh. She leaned in and whispered, "Don't worry. My parents will love you."

He took her hand in his and brought it to his lips. He caught Melanie and Charles watching him, and buried his feelings about them deep within him, along with everything else he felt bad about but had no way of changing.

Chelle asked Melanie about Jace, and that started a catching-up-on-news conversation between the two women that lasted the duration of the ride to the Landons' ranch. When they arrived, Charles waited beside the limo for Mason. He looked surprisingly apologetic.

"Mace, I had to ask."

Mason shook his head and turned away from his friend. "No, Charles, you didn't."

Chapter Fourteen

Watching Mason pass a plate of potatoes around her parents' dining room table felt as surreal as the entire last two weeks had. Charles and Melanie had returned to their home, saying they had promised David they would pick Jace up early. Chelle thought it had more to do with whatever Charles and Mason had said to each other back at the airport, but she'd let them go without protest. Dinner with her parents would be tricky enough without adding another layer of tension to it.

After an initial awkward few moments in which her mother had hugged Mason for too long and her father had given him a handshake that made him wince, Chelle's parents had told her and Mason they had just enough time to freshen up before dinner. As she'd predicted, her parents were adamant that she and Mason stay at their home. They'd set up a room for Mason on the far side of the house, just beyond her parents' room. Her father had not-so-subtly mentioned he'd never fixed the creaking boards in that hallway, and any late-night wandering to the bathroom would likely wake the whole house. Her eyes had sought Mason's, and they'd shared a look that had them both choking back their laughter.

They'd almost lost it a second time when Chelle's mother had asked them if they'd flown straight there or stopped anywhere along the way. She'd said, "Galveston is such a beautiful city and worth the detour. Nice shops there, too."

That time, Chelle had not met Mason's eyes. She never would have been able to keep her composure if she had. She was already beating back hot memories from their flight over.

While spooning peas onto her plate, Chelle's mother said, "Everyone is heading over to Mrs. Nicholson's at eight in the morning. You two should turn in early; you both look tired."

Chelle choked on the water she had been sipping.

Mason added smoothly, "Good idea. Traveling is exhausting."

Chelle's father cut into his steak and said, "I heard you flew in on a private plane. California sure is generous with their senators."

Mason answered without hesitation. "I would never use public money for personal purposes. I'm fortunate that the investments I made when I was younger allow me the freedom to choose how I travel."

Her father harrumphed. "Acting and politics, two careers I can't say I hold much admiration for. And you're a Democrat?"

"Dad," Chelle said in protest and looked to her mother in an appeal for help.

Her mother gave her less sympathy than she'd hoped for. "Chelle, when you bring a man home and say you're marrying him, you can't expect your father not to want to get to know him."

Flashing that smooth smile Chelle had seen him use many times before, Mason said, "I am a Democrat, but I won't hold your Republican affiliation against you. Texas used to be a Democratic state. Who knows, you may find yourself voting that way again."

"It'll be a cold day in hell before I vote for some bleeding-heart liberal. All you do is pass more sissified laws. Seat belts. Helmets. I'm waiting for the day my cousins up north start covering their kids in Bubble Wrap before letting them outside to play. In my day, kids fell down. And yes, they got hurt, but you know what? They learned how not to fall down. How the hell can a kid learn how to survive if they spend all day on a damn couch?"

The rant was not a new one. Her father was a Vietnam veteran. He believed in family, God, and country, and his views probably hadn't changed in the last fifty years. There was no use arguing with him; he'd seen men die fighting for freedom, and he didn't like anyone telling him what to do. Chelle's mother told her she had a lot of her father in her, and Chelle didn't mind the comparison. Her father had marched for civil rights reform. He believed in freedom for all, regardless of religious, racial, or lifestyle differences. You just couldn't tell him he needed to wear a helmet when he rode a horse.

Chelle bit back a smile as she remembered what he'd said to a man who had applied for a job at the ranch and asked if a helmet was required for riding. Her father had said, "You know what I would do if one of my hands wore one? I'd beat the tar out of him myself. If you're so afraid of falling, get your ass off my horses."

Mason cut into his steak and said blandly, "Some couches are quite dangerous. They have those levers on the side and snap into place. A person could easily lose a finger."

Her father opened his mouth to say something, appeared to realize Mason was poking a little fun at him, and snapped his mouth shut.

Chelle quickly interceded by explaining the merits of the water bill Mason was working on. She wanted her father to see the good he was doing.

Her father laid down his knife and studied Mason. "That can't be a popular stand to take."

Mason's expression hardened. "It's not, but the right thing to do is often not the easiest. My second term ends in two years. I can't run again for this office, but I can use my remaining time to get some long-term policies put in place that will hopefully avert what could be one of our nation's largest man-made disasters if we allow it to go unchecked."

"We struggle with similar issues here. So"—her father continued his cross-examination—"what are your plans for after you leave the senate? Can you see yourself here in Texas?"

"Dad," Chelle protested again. "We haven't discussed that yet."

"Well, you need to," her father countered. "Marriage isn't something you should jump in and out of like so many people do today. I want to know that the two of you have thought this through. Are you planning on having children? Have you talked about if Chelle is going to continue to work? She left here thinking she wanted to find her dream job and came back with you. I want to know what else she found out there."

Chelle's mother put her hand on her husband's shoulder. "Roger, don't you think you're being too hard on them? If my father had asked us where we wanted to be, we would have said together. Give them time to figure everything out. We've raised a smart daughter. Trust her to make good choices."

Roger gave Mason a long look. "I trust our daughter; it's him I'm not sure about yet."

Mason held his tongue and met Chelle's eyes. She shot him a grateful look. A week ago she would have been writhing internally from guilt as she lied to her parents. But now she didn't feel guilty at all. Their actual engagement might not be real, but how she felt about Mason was. "Dad, I wouldn't have brought Mason home to meet you if I didn't think he was the most amazing man I've ever known."

A funny, pained expression passed over Mason's face.

Roger's eyes narrowed and he asked, "What does your father do for a living, Mason?"

"I don't know. He and I don't speak."

Chelle knew that wasn't an easy admission for Mason to make. She put her hand on his and gave it a squeeze. She wanted to protect him from the questions, but she also understood what her mother had said about letting them get to know each other.

"And your mother?" her father asked gruffly.

"She died when I was eighteen," Mason said, his tone devoid of emotion.

Her father's expression softened. "I'm sorry to hear that."

Mason shrugged a shoulder. "It was a long time ago."

Roger nodded, then threw his napkin down beside his plate. "Bryn, dinner was wonderful as always. If you don't mind, I'd like to show Mason around. It's early enough for us to get in a ride before sundown."

"That sounds perfect. It'll give Chelle and me time to catch up," Bryn answered.

Her father and Mason stood, and Chelle panicked. She interjected quickly, "Dad, I'm sure Mason doesn't ride."

Roger turned to Mason. "Do you?"

Mason's unreadable smile was back. "Of course."

"Then let's go," Roger said and led the way out of the dining room.

Mason winked at her as he followed her father. Chelle had no idea what that meant. "Mom, we have to stop them. What if Mason said he can ride just because he didn't want to say no to Dad?"

Her mother started clearing the dishes from the table. "Grab the glasses. I'll take the plates. And then you need to tell me why you're marrying a man you don't know all that much about. Are you pregnant?"

Chelle gathered the glasses and followed her mother into the kitchen. "No. Oh, Mom. Did you ever do something that feels right and wrong at the same time?"

"He's not married to someone else already, is he?" Bryn asked while leading the way back to retrieve more dishes.

"No, nothing like that."

A moment later, they were back in the kitchen. Her mother was washing the dishes, and Chelle was drying them. "Well, speak, child. I'm listening."

Chelle dried another dish and stacked it in the cupboard. "I'm happy, Mom. Nothing happened the way I would have planned it, but does that make it bad? I want to be with Mason, and he wants to be with me. Can't that be enough?"

Bryn took a break from washing the dishes and wiped her hands on a towel. "We're happy you found someone, Chelle, but your father's not the only one who is worried. You don't have to rush into anything. Take your time. If this is the man you're meant to be with, it'll happen."

Chelle turned and leaned back against the counter. "If you're so worried, why are you having a party for us tomorrow?"

Bryn kissed her daughter's forehead and said, "You're our only child, and if you love Mason, then we love him, too, and that's something to celebrate, don't you think?"

Chelle threw her arms around her mother and hugged her. "It is. How did I end up with the best parents in the world?"

Her mother wiped away a tear and smoothed her hands on her apron before turning back to the sink. "Well, you didn't do it by slacking on your chores. We'll have company in and out of here all day tomorrow. Let's get this place cleaned up."

Chelle picked up the towel again and dried another dish. "I don't have a solid plan about anything, Mom. I'm twenty-five, and I feel like my whole life is up in the air. Sometimes I feel free. Sometimes I'm downright terrified."

Her mother paused again and met her eyes. "I've seen you make tough choices in the past, but I've never heard you say you've regretted them. You'll be fine, Chelle. Keep following that beautiful heart of yours, and you'll end up where you're supposed to be."

Chelle nodded, glad she'd come home. She hoped Mason was enjoying himself as much as she was. "You don't think Dad would put Mason in danger, do you?"

The quick *no* Chelle had hoped to hear didn't come. Instead, her mother rinsed the last dish off and said, "Why don't we go check on them?"

Mason took a long, hard look at the horse Chelle's father had asked his ranch hand to saddle for him. The mare was swaybacked and insultingly aged; she was in her thirties if she was a day old. He could feel Roger watching his reaction and knew he was being tested.

Had Mason not learned to ride at one of the summer camps his parents had sent him to, he would have accepted that mount. His parents had cultivated skills in Mason they thought would help him become a star. He'd taken fencing, self-defense, riding, and acting lessons as early on as he could remember. It hadn't particularly mattered if he enjoyed them or not, although he had. Especially riding. The rider and the horse worked together, or they failed. Mason's instructors had said he was a natural.

He hadn't ridden since before his mother died. Temptation spurred him to see if he could still do it. Mason looked away from the old mare being led toward him and scanned the paddocks. "Do you have anything younger? A little more challenging to ride?"

He spotted a well-muscled brown horse in a round pen. "How about him?"

Roger shook his head. "You wouldn't want him. He requires an experienced rider."

Mason walked over to the pen and looked the horse over. "I'd like to try him."

"Are you sure I can't talk you out of it?" Roger asked in a dry tone.

"I'm sure," Mason said with growing confidence.

Roger told the ranch hand to saddle the younger horse. The man said, "Boss, isn't that the horse you're sending over to Tony because—"

Roger cut the man off. "Saddle him up."

"Yes, boss." The man gave Mason a look and shrugged.

Mason was no fool. He had a pretty good idea that the horse being saddled for him had issues. He could have confronted Roger and gotten him to admit it. He could just as easily have refused to ride the horse.

But he had a feeling Chelle's father wouldn't have respected him for choosing either one of those options.

Mason decided to get up on that horse, and if he were thrown, he would get back on. He was going to prove to Roger he was not out of place on that ranch. Exactly why Roger's opinion mattered so much wasn't something Mason was about to analyze. It just did.

When the ranch hand returned with the bay, Mason walked over and laid his hand on the horse's neck. "What's his name?"

"We call him Fury, but on paper his name's Prancer. The breeder's daughter named him. She thought he had a cute trot. He didn't make it as a family horse, though."

Mason looked into the horse's eyes. He didn't see craziness there; he saw anxiety. So he spoke softly and slowly. "Well, Prancer, you need to consider rebranding yourself. I can't say either name fits you. How about Tango? Would you like me to call you that?"

"What's he doing?" the ranch hand asked.

"He's having a conversation with the damn horse," Roger answered.

"You think he can ride?"

"He says he can."

"You want me to call Doc Stevens and have him on standby?"

Mason tuned the two men out and said, "Tango, I'll make you a deal. Don't throw me, and I will make sure they change your name." With that, he swung himself up into the saddle and waited.

The horse danced nervously beneath him, but Mason left the reins slack. He relaxed in his seat and let the horse settle. Like riding a bike, his ability to communicate with horses came back to him. He could hear his trainer telling him to keep his commands firm, but his hands light.

Mason didn't consider himself a horse whisperer, but he could read people and animals. He would bet the horse below him had been spoiled by his previous owner and allowed to pick up some bad habits. Habits cowboys would have no tolerance for. If he was right, the horse wasn't angry; he was confused and frustrated. The rules had all changed for him, and Mason could imagine how the horse would respond to being harshly reined in. Mason would buck, too.

He asked the horse to walk and kept that in mind. He ignored the dance and focused on guiding the horse to where he wanted to go. The horse took off at a run, and Mason let him. He ran that horse down the path along the side of the barn, across the field, and back. When the horse began to slow, he pushed him to run more. Only when they came around the large barn for the second time did Mason ask the horse to drop down to a walk again.

And the horse did. Feeling exhilarated, Mason gave the horse a hearty pat on the neck and rode up beside Chelle's father. "Are you saddling up?"

Roger's face split into a smile for the first time that day. "Well, I'll be damned. That horse may not need Tony Carlton after all." He turned to his ranch hand. "Tack Checkers up for me. Looks like we're going for a ride."

After the ranch hand was out of earshot, Roger said, "I was sure I'd see you fall on your ass, son, but I'm glad you didn't. Chelle needs a strong man she can respect. That doesn't mean I agree with all the tomfoolery I've read about you in the press, but I'm sure that's all behind you now."

"Yes, sir," Mason said, treating the man with more deference than he'd ever shown, even with his own father. There was something about Roger that made a man want to stand straighter around him.

"Roger Wilton Landon, tell me you did not put my future son-in-law on a horse you said was dangerous." Chelle's mother's voice rang out from the porch steps.

Mason choked back a laugh and avoided Roger's eyes. They'd gotten to a good place he didn't want to spoil.

"Oh my God, Dad. He could have been killed." Chelle closed the distance between them.

Roger's horse arrived, and he swung himself into the saddle. "Don't get yourselves all lathered up. In fact, since you two are out here, do you want to join us? I thought we'd ride down to the summer pasture."

Chelle looked up at Mason. "Are you all right?"

Roger made a disgusted sound. "Don't coddle the man. He's a fine rider."

"He is?" Chelle asked in awe. A huge smile spread across his face. "Of course he is." She turned to her mother. "Mom? Do you want to go?"

Bryn waved a finger at her husband, but nodded. "You are so lucky he didn't get hurt. Come on, Chelle. Clover will be happy to see you." She looked back at her husband. "We'll be two minutes. I want everyone still alive when I come back."

Chelle and her mother led their horses into the barn while two ranch hands rushed to help them. Roger cleared his throat and said, "If she's still mad at me later, I'll apologize. You remember that, son. Pride isn't strength; it's weakness. There's no shame in saying you're sorry so you don't have to sleep in the barn."

"Yes, sir," Mason responded automatically while he tried to figure out why Roger's words had touched him so deeply. Mason wanted to believe people could be as genuinely good as Chelle's family appeared.

He wanted to, but believing wasn't his strong suit.

Chapter Fifteen

Later that night, Chelle and Mason sat side by side on the porch swing. Chelle couldn't remember ever having a better day in her life. She looked down at her hand laced through Mason's and thought if she died right then, no undertaker would be able to wipe the smile off her face. "You survived meeting my parents," Chelle said.

Mason tightened his grip on her hand. "It wasn't hard. They're nice people."

Chelle chuckled. "Nice? My dad did everything but ask you for a blood sample at dinner."

Mason smiled. "He wanted to make sure I was good enough for his daughter."

"How did he get you up on that horse?" Chelle asked with a shake of her head.

"I chose it."

"Dad should have told you he considered Fury dangerous."

Mason shrugged. "Tango, and I would have gotten on him anyway."

"Tango, is it? I don't understand men sometimes. Was it really worth risking breaking your neck?"

"Yes," Mason said simply.

Chelle laid her head on Mason's shoulder. "I used to ride with my parents all the time when I was younger, but I haven't in a while. I'm glad we did tonight."

Mason turned his head and nuzzled her hair before saying, "Me too."

"Where did you learn to ride? I pictured you growing up in a city."

He shifted as if the topic of his past made him uncomfortable. "I did, but my parents wanted to prepare me for any role I might get in a movie."

"Did you always know you wanted to be an actor?"

Mason was quiet for a moment. "I didn't have a choice. My parents didn't come from money. I don't know what their finances were before I started working, but I don't think they were very good. My mother used to say people would stop and stare at me when I was a baby. They'd tell her I was the most beautiful child they'd ever seen or that I belonged in commercials or on TV."

"It must have been devastating for you when she died."

Mason stared out into the darkness and said, "Yes. It was senseless, and it was difficult not to resent her for that."

"You don't think she killed herself, do you?"

Mason shrugged. "I don't know. I'll never know. My mother was prone to depression, and she closely linked her identity to my success. If I was doing well, she was on top of the world. If I failed at something, she couldn't handle it. She and my father wanted to control every decision I made, right down to what I wore each day. It was too much. That's why I fired my father. I didn't want to hate them, and I was starting to."

"And then your mother died."

"Yes."

Chelle's eyes filled with tears. "You must have felt responsible. You were too young to realize it wasn't your fault."

When Mason fell quiet, Chelle decided to change the subject. She didn't want the dark cloud of the past to mar what she hoped had been an amazing day for him. "Tomorrow is going to be crazy. Most of the town will probably be at Mrs. Nicholson's. Some will come because they want to congratulate us, and some because they're curious. Either way, prepare yourself for a whole lot of handshaking."

"I'm used to that," Mason said with some humor.

Chelle rocked back and forth in silence, letting herself simply enjoy being next to Mason. What had started as a game at Sarah's wedding had grown into something real. She could picture being married to Mason. It was easy enough to imagine herself standing beside him in Sacramento as well as raising children with him in Fort Mavis.

She let out a long, slow breath and admitted to herself that she had fallen completely, irreversibly in love with him. She loved how confident he was in public and how he let her see beyond that when they were alone. She loved how easily they could make each other laugh or turn each other on. She would have loved him even if he hadn't known a horse from a donkey, but watching him bond with her father and the ranch hands was a little piece of heaven on earth.

Tracing the edge of Mason's thumb with hers, Chelle said, "I'm sorry you and Charles are having issues. I get the feeling it's over me, and I don't want to come between you two."

Mason lifted his arm, wrapped it around Chelle's shoulders, and kissed her forehead. "I've certainly done enough to deserve his opinion of me."

Chelle voiced what she knew he couldn't. "But it hurts."

He made a sound deep in his chest.

Chelle raised her head and said, "Melanie thinks Charles is afraid we've taken this game too far, but it's not a game to me."

Mason tensed beside her.

She knew she shouldn't, but she couldn't stop herself from saying, "Mason, I love—"

Mason stood abruptly. "I have a few e-mails I need to answer before I zonk out tonight. Thank God for smartphones." He whipped open the door to the house and said, "Good night."

"Good night," Chelle said sadly as she watched him retreat into the house without even kissing her good night. She sank deeper into the swing and closed her eyes.

She thought about his mother and how deeply he must have felt her loss. She wondered if that was why he'd lost touch with his father, and her heart went out to both of them. Death had a way of either bringing people together or driving them away from each other. Sarah had described how the latter had happened to her family after her little brother had drowned. So much guilt. So much pain.

Mason probably felt he didn't deserve love. He was wrong.

She thought back to her first impression of him and how cocky he had come across. Like her town, Mason had layers. She believed with all her heart if she kept peeling them back, she would find a man who loved her as much as she loved him.

Once he stops running.

Mason paced his small bedroom in the Landon home. His heart was beating wildly in his chest. He felt hot and cold at the same time and more than a little sick.

Chelle loves me.

I let this go too far. I've been selfish and refused to listen to any of Charles's warnings. I told myself I could have what I wanted without anyone getting hurt.

The truth was in her eyes. Their engagement was real to her.

Fuck.

He'd told her it was temporary, and she'd agreed to those terms. Why did she have to take their relationship further than they'd agreed to go?

He rubbed his forehead in frustration. *Because she comes from a good family. Because she doesn't understand there is no such thing as unicorns and happily ever afters.*

He'd walked away because he hadn't wanted to tell her he didn't love her. He hadn't wanted to disappoint her. The memory of the look in her eyes when he'd bolted for the house tore at him. She should have been angry. Instead, she'd had that damned sympathetic look on her face that he'd seen before—like she wanted to hug his pain away.

She'd looked at him the same way when he'd told her how his mother had died. *I don't know why I told her anything.* Chelle had a way of getting him to open up about things he'd never discussed with anyone.

He should hate that about her, but he didn't.

Being with her was fucking amazing. Whether it was walking into a party with her and knowing she was about to charm the socks off every person in the room, or waking up beside her and instantly feeling better about the day before him. Yes, they were a good match, in and out of bed, but that didn't mean he was ready to vow to spend the rest of his life with her.

By falling in love with him, Chelle had ruined everything.

Mason sat on the edge of the bed and put his head in his hands. He couldn't see any choice other than breaking it off with her. And soon. But not tomorrow. He couldn't do that to her. Not in front of her family and the whole town.

I'll do it back in Sacramento. Just like we had planned. Only I'll find a way to make her think it was her idea.

He punched the bed beside him.

As much as he tried to fight it, the truth could not be denied. He didn't want to break up with her. His gut twisted painfully at the idea of never seeing her again. What he wanted was a time machine that could take him back to before she'd said she loved him. Back to when he'd felt completely in control and had prided himself on his indifference.

I was happier as an asshole.

He shook his head. *That's not true. I wasn't happy. But I wasn't this miserable, either.*

Under any other circumstances he would have called Charles, but he didn't want to hear his friend's opinion on this problem.

He knew he needed to end it with Chelle before she fell harder for him.

He wanted to forget she'd said anything.

He flopped backward onto the bed.

Charles is right about one thing—I went too far.

Chapter Sixteen

It was hard not to worry a little when Mason joined her family for breakfast and took a seat without giving her a good-morning kiss. She told herself it was simply because he didn't want to make her feel uncomfortable in front of her family, but he was also having difficulty looking her in the eye. She hadn't known him long, but she'd spent enough time with him to be able to read his mood.

The kitchen was overflowing with relatives who couldn't wait until the party to meet Mason. He smiled as he greeted each of them, but she knew that smile. It was the one he used with the public. She called it his game face. Men accepted it, women fawned over it, but Chelle knew it was an act.

When their eyes met across the kitchen and he flashed that fake bright smile at her, she knew something was definitely wrong. There wasn't time to speak to him privately, though. Her parents' house was a bustle of preparation and congratulations.

Before she knew it, she and Mason were in a truck they'd borrowed from her parents and were heading down the driveway. Mason looked perfectly at home driving the twenty-year-old Ford. Chelle reached out, took Mason's hand in hers, and gave him directions to Mrs. Nicholson's house.

He frowned, then turned his head to meet her eyes. The torment Chelle saw there tore at her heart. *I shouldn't have brought up his mother last night. I put that look in his eyes.*

"I'm sorry," she said gently, her eyes shining with tears.

He groaned and gave her hand a squeeze. "Don't be. I'm an ass."

Chelle chuckled. "Sometimes."

He laughed with her and brought her hand up to his lips. "You could have hesitated a little before agreeing."

Chelle raised her head and met his eyes again. "Your ego can take it."

He cocked an eyebrow in concession, then his expression became more serious. "Everything will be perfect today, Chelle. I'll make sure it is."

"I'm not worried."

His expression darkened again, and he seemed to want to say more, but they arrived at Mrs. Nicholson's house and parked beside a slew of other trucks.

One of Chelle's cousins was beside them instantly, telling Mason where the men were assembling their tools and equipment. Mason glanced back at her, and Chelle forced herself to smile and wave. Whatever he wanted to tell her would likely have to wait until they flew back to Sacramento in the morning.

Sarah appeared at her side, wide awake and as chipper as usual. "What a beautiful day. I love Fort Mavis. We don't have anything like this in Rhode Island. What an incredible way to turn a celebration into something that benefits the community. How can you stand being away from here?"

Chelle looked around before answering, "It's surprisingly easier than you'd think. Don't get me wrong—I love it here, but I need more. I enjoy meeting people I don't know and seeing things I've never seen.

I like getting lost in a new city and trying foods I've never even heard of. These last two weeks have been . . . magical."

Sarah nodded toward Mason, who was donning a tool belt and climbing up a ladder to join several other men on the roof. "That might also have something to do with who you've spent your time with."

Chelle blushed. "I can't argue with that. Mason is everything I've always wanted in a man. He's funny. He's kind. He's amazing in bed. Even my parents like him."

Sarah gave Chelle a quick hug. "Look at you. You go off to California to meet your fake fiancé and come back with a real one."

Melanie joined them with a yawn. "Jace was so excited to come and help out today, he woke us up at five." She looked Chelle over. "How did dinner go last night?"

. Chelle watched Mason help strip the roof of the old shingles. "Better than I dared hope. He got along so well with my parents that we all went for a trail ride before bed."

"That's great," Melanie said slowly. "I'm glad Charles is up there next to Mason. I know he feels badly about yesterday."

"He should," Chelle volleyed back.

Sarah put a hand on her hip. "What did my brother do now?"

Melanie made a face, then admitted, "He had it out with Mason over Chelle. His heart is in the right place, but he could have been gentler with his approach."

"Mason has been nothing but wonderful to me," Chelle said firmly.

Sarah cut in. "Charles will just have to understand that love happens. If Mason and Chelle want to make their fake engagement real, he should be happy for them."

Melanie flashed a look at Chelle. "Did something change since yesterday? Did Mason actually say he wanted the engagement to be a real one?"

Chelle stuck her hands in the front pockets of her jeans and looked away. "Not exactly."

"Did he say he loves you?" Melanie pushed.

Chelle pursed her lips in anger. She didn't answer. She didn't have to. She and Melanie both knew he hadn't.

"He has to. Why would he be here if he didn't?" Sarah asked.

Melanie pointed across the yard to the news crew filming from the other side of the street. "Charles said Mason has been doing really well in the polls since he's made a big deal out of being engaged to a small-town girl. His advisers had been telling him to clean up his image, and being with Chelle is helping him do that."

Chelle shook her head. "Mason told my father he's not running for the senate again."

In a slightly apologetic tone, Melanie added, "There have been rumors Mason could run for governor. They say the only thing holding him back is his reputation. He could be using you, Chelle. I don't want to believe he's capable of anything like that, but he sure jumped at the idea of pretending to be engaged. Men don't do that. Not men without an agenda, anyway."

Chelle's hands went cold, and she brought them both to her mouth. Could Mason be using her? Every fiber of her being said no. Mason paused from pulling off shingles. He wiped the sweat from his forehead, then turned and sought her out in the crowd. Chelle waved at him, and he waved back. This time, his smile was the special one he only gave her.

"Mason would never do that." With that, Chelle walked away from her friends toward where the women were setting up for the party that would follow.

She heard Sarah say, "He might love her."

She wished she'd missed Melanie's response: "But what if he doesn't?"

Mason downed an ice-cold beer and crushed the can in his hand. He laid it on the table beside the heaping plate of ribs Chelle had brought him. Hours of manual labor and his interactions with the men of Fort Mavis had left him feeling better about everything.

No one looked at him like they feared he would sleep with their wives. They didn't throw his past in his face. They cared that he'd worked as hard as they had and that he'd done right by one of the women of their town. Their approval of him filled him with a pride he couldn't explain. He liked who he was in that crazy little town.

He'd lost count of how many people had told him he was a lucky bastard to be marrying a woman like Chelle. All day long, he'd heard stories about her, from when she'd hidden the class turtle in her pocket because she'd thought he missed his friends in the pond to how she'd cried the day she'd decided not to go to college in Boston.

She brought her own plate of food to the spot beside him and sat down with a smile and a tired sigh. "All this celebrating is hard work, but Mrs. Nicholson has a new roof, no one died in the process, and there is still beer in the cooler. Today's a success."

Mason leaned over and kissed her warmly. She brought both hands up to frame his face and kissed him back.

"Now that's what I'm talking about," someone said.

Chelle laughed and broke the kiss off. "Family. What can you do?"

Mason looked around at all the people who were smiling and cheering, and his chest constricted painfully. He gazed back down at Chelle and thought, *I want this to be real. I want to love her.*

Mason grabbed Chelle by the shoulders and kissed her with all the pent-up emotions running through him. There was nothing standing between him and what he wanted: a future with Chelle. Why couldn't he let himself go and have the kind of faith in her that she had in him?

A hand squeezed one of his shoulders tightly, and her father's voice boomed, "There'll be plenty of time for that after the wedding."

Mason lifted his head and smiled unapologetically at Roger. "You did say you wanted grandchildren."

A hush fell over the crowd as they waited to hear Roger's response. He said, "You ever hear of a shotgun wedding? Around here, not all the grooms make it to the altar." He winked.

"Dad," Chelle said and rolled her eyes.

Mason chuckled. "I'll keep that in mind, sir."

Music began to play, and everyone's attention moved from Chelle and Mason to the grassy dance floor. Mason pulled Chelle over to sit on his lap. He didn't want to lose her. If that meant making his bond with her legal, that's what he would do. "We need to talk."

She studied his face for a minute. "About?"

"About us. Let's go for a drive tonight. Just you and me."

With her arms wrapped around his neck, Chelle kissed him lightly. "I'd like that. I'd like that a lot."

Mason's phone rang. He recognized the number as Ruby's, but didn't answer. He'd have to explain to Ruby he couldn't be her arm candy anymore. There was only one woman he wanted to be with, and she needed to hear him say what he'd been too afraid to admit until then.

Chelle stood and pulled on Mason's hand. "Come dance with me." There was a slow country ballad playing.

He stood and twirled her before him. "Absolutely, they're playing our song."

"Do we have a song?"

He led her toward the dance floor. "We do now."

After several songs, Mason and Chelle conceded they were both getting tired. Hand in hand, they were walking back to their table when Mason's phone rang again. He wouldn't have answered it, but it was Millie.

"Mason, I would never interrupt your weekend, but I received a call from Ruby Skye, and she sounded . . . out of it. She was crying and talking crazy. I told her I'd try to get in touch with you. I've never heard her like this before. I didn't know what to do except call you."

"You did the right thing, Millie," Mason said abruptly and hung up. The wonder of the day crashed and shattered around him in a million irreparable shards. No matter how far he ran, his past would find him and pull him down.

Chelle stepped in front of him and asked, "What's wrong, Mason?"

He answered absently, "I don't know. I need to make a call, Chelle. I'm sorry." He walked away from her without saying more. He knew she was hurt that he had closed her out of what was going on, but he didn't want her to be part of this.

When Ruby answered, she slurred his name. "Mason."

"Ruby, what did you take? Where are you?"

"I'm at my house in Malibu. Everything is falling apart, Mason, and I don't know what to do. The pills don't help. I took one. Maybe two. I just want to sleep, but they're not working."

"What happened?"

"I came home from the shoot in Australia, and Brady was in bed with my housekeeper. The fucking housekeeper. I threw them both out. Now I'm all alone." She started to sob. "I can't sleep when I'm alone."

"Ruby, I'm calling someone to go over there."

"No," she cried out. "No one can know about this. I could lose everything. I just landed a movie deal. Those don't come easy anymore. They say I'm too old for many of the parts. I'm thirty, not ninety. Mason, you can't tell anyone about this. Promise me you won't."

Mason clenched his hand at his side. "I promise. What do you want me to do?"

"Can you come over?"

"I'm in Texas, and I'm engaged."

Ruby started crying again. "I don't want to fuck you, but I can't be alone tonight. I'm afraid if I am, I won't be here tomorrow. Have you ever felt that way, Mason? You start thinking maybe it would be better if you fell asleep and never woke up?"

"Shit, Ruby. I'm sending Millie over. Don't do anything."

"Millie won't leak it to the press, will she?"

"Millie? Millie's a vault."

"I'm so sorry. I don't have anyone else, Mason."

"I'll be there before morning. Let Millie in when she rings you. Her next call will be to the police if you don't."

"I will. Thank you, Mason. You're really coming?"

"Yes," Mason said tersely and hung up. Guilt from the past swirled within him. He looked back at Chelle, who was anxiously waiting for him to return to her. He couldn't tell her about Ruby. If she told anyone and it somehow got to the press, it might send Ruby off the edge she was already teetering on.

Ruby wasn't exaggerating how she felt. He'd known her long enough to believe the desperation in her voice. She was hitting rock bottom, a scary place to go alone. He remembered that feeling all too well, and he'd be damned if he'd stand by and do nothing while she followed in his mother's footsteps.

Chelle had said his mother's death hadn't been his fault. His head knew she was right, but that didn't stop him from hating his mother for dying, himself for not knowing how depressed she'd become, and his father for not saving his family from the dark path they'd all gone down.

He cared about Ruby, but that wasn't the only thing that was driving his decision to go to her. He needed to get her the help he wished he'd gotten his mother. No, it wouldn't change anything that had happened, but that didn't matter. The past had risen up and was tearing into him again.

He looked around at the people who had welcomed him into their town, and wondered what they'd think of him if they knew the self-destructive lifestyle he'd lived, how close he'd come to being Ruby.

Chelle thought she loved him, but she didn't know this side of him. She belonged in a place like Fort Mavis, surrounded by people who gathered for scrapbooking parties. She deserved better than whatever he would find at Ruby's house. Better than him.

He took Chelle aside and said, "Something urgent came up. I have to go back to California tonight."

She took his hand in hers. "I'll go with you."

He shook his head and gently removed his hand from hers. "I need to do this alone."

"What happened?"

"I can't tell you."

She chewed her bottom lip. "How long will you be gone?"

"I don't know."

"Will you call me?"

"If I can."

Chelle opened her mouth, closed it, then said quietly, "You make it very difficult to believe in you."

He kissed her lips with tenderness and said, "It's better for both of us if you don't."

With that, he walked away from Chelle and asked one of the men for a ride to the airport. He would use the time on the flight back to California to distance himself from his emotions. He wouldn't let himself wonder if Chelle was upset.

He was going back to face his past. He would either beat it or lose himself to it. Either way, it was not something he could explain to Chelle.

Chapter Seventeen

Chelle sat on the back bumper of a truck and watched Mason leave with one of her cousins. She didn't want to get upset in front of her family and friends, but she couldn't help herself. She wiped away tears as they flowed down her cheeks.

David sat down beside her and handed her a napkin. "I can drive you home if you want."

Chelle wiped her face and shook her head. "I'll be fine. Why can't anything stay perfect? Does life always have to even out? You're not allowed real joy unless it's followed by a kick to the crotch?"

"You picked a tough man to fall in love with, Chelle. Seems like that man has a dark past. One he tries to hide."

With a deep, shaking breath, Chelle calmed herself enough that she no longer needed the napkin. "I don't care what he did." She sniffed. "Well, unless he killed people. I couldn't get over that. But I get that he made bad choices. He told me. And he told me why. He's a good man, David. He's just lost."

"Where'd he go?"

"He wouldn't tell me."

"Is he coming back?"

"He didn't say."

"You deserve better than that, Chelle."

"You know that corny expression about someone being someone else's world? I never understood that until I met Mason. When I'm with him everything is different, better. Nothing else matters; I know I'm where I belong. A feeling that strong can't be wrong, can it?"

David sighed. "When it comes to love, I wouldn't say I'm qualified to give advice."

Chelle turned to face David. "Lucy's still engaged, isn't she? Did you tell her how you feel about her?"

David tipped his Stetson lower. "She made her choice."

"So that's it? You're giving up without a fight?"

David shrugged. "I respect her decision."

Chelle hopped off the back of the truck. "I didn't take you for a quitter, David. Go tell her you love her, and see just how happy she is or isn't with that fiancé of hers."

David pushed his hat back. "I might do that, Chelle. And if Mason doesn't come back, he's a damn fool."

Chelle straightened her shoulders and said, "He'll be back," with confidence.

David headed back to help the men clear away the trash from the party. Sarah and Melanie took his place beside Chelle.

Sarah asked cheerfully, "Where'd you hide Mason? We're thinking about making a bonfire."

Chelle let out a long, sad breath. "He had to go back to California."

Looking concerned, Melanie asked, "Did you two have a fight?"

"No. There was something he needed to handle back home."

Sarah put a hand on Chelle's shoulder. "He's a senator. He probably gets called back for all kinds of emergencies."

"True, but he didn't want me to go back with him."

Sarah waved her other hand in the air with flair. "He was being considerate. Your whole family is here and celebrating with you. He probably didn't want to take you away from that. Did he say when he would be back?"

Chelle felt her eyes tearing up again and blinked quickly. "Can we talk about something else?"

"Oh boy," Melanie said. "Here come your parents."

Just when I thought it couldn't get worse.

Her father pinned her down with a look that told her he wasn't pleased. "Did I see Mason leave?"

"Yes, Dad. There was an emergency back in California."

"Must have been something mighty important for him to go without even saying good-bye or thanking anyone."

"I really don't want to talk about it." A tear rolled down her cheek, and she hastily wiped it away.

Her mother linked her arm with her husband's. "Let's not discuss anything more with everyone watching. We're all set to go home. Chelle, would you like to ride with us?"

Chelle thought about how she'd feel sitting in her room all by herself and shook her head. "No, I'll be along later."

As her parents walked away, she heard her father say, "I'll kill the bastard if he hurts my baby."

Charles and Tony walked over to join them, and Charles asked, "Did Mason leave?"

It was the straw that broke the camel's back. She stormed up to Charles and snapped, "Yes, he did. He left. Don't ask me why. Don't ask if he's coming back. I don't know. All I do know is that whatever happens between Mason and me is none of your damn business, Charles."

He looked at Melanie, who blushed and made an apologetic face. "I may have told her you were worried about how it would work out."

Chelle continued her rant. "Mason has been nothing but good to me. I don't know what awful thing he did to you, Charles, but I thought you were good friends. You made him feel awful about coming here with me. And that wasn't right. I may not have known him as long as you have, but I understand him a whole lot better than you. He wouldn't leave me unless it was something very important. I believe that. And if you don't, could you all kindly keep your thoughts to yourself?"

Tony raised his hands in front of his chest in mock surrender. Sarah elbowed her husband in reprimand.

Melanie linked her hand with Charles's. She looked up at him and said, "She's right, you know. It's none of our business. Charles, you said yourself you were a different man before you met me. Love might do the same for Mason. You don't know what's in his heart."

Charles pulled his fiancée into his arms. "I spoke to Mason while we were working on the roof. I'm not proud of some of the things I said to him yesterday, and I told him that. He has been a very good friend to me for a very long time. I've never seen him look at anyone the way he looks at Chelle. If that's not love, it's damn close to it. But I don't know if it will be enough."

Melanie asked, "Enough to do what?"

Chelle answered, "For him to put the past behind him. I know how his mother died, Charles. He told me."

Charles added, "Then you know it shaped who he is. He doesn't let anyone get close. He bolted today. If he doesn't call you, it may be over."

Chelle heard the warning, but she trusted what her heart was telling her. "He wouldn't do that."

"I've seen him—" Charles started to say, but Chelle cut him off.

"To *me*. He wouldn't do that to me. Now, if you don't mind, I'm going to finish helping everyone clean up, and then I'm going home."

When Chelle finally walked up the steps of her parents' home, it was late, but the lights were still on inside. Instead of going inside she sat on the porch swing and tried not to succumb to the doubt that was nipping at her heels.

Mason hadn't called her.

She'd tried to call him, but he hadn't answered.

She sat on the swing, telling herself he had a good reason for both.

The screen door opened, and her parents came out to the porch. They each took a seat on either side of her.

"I don't want to talk about it," Chelle said when the silence became unbearable.

"You don't have to," her mother answered. "But we love you, and we're not going anywhere."

Chelle wiped at one of her eyes. "Dad, I know you want to say something about Mason, but please don't."

Her father put his arm around her shoulders and pulled her against him. "I fought in a war and it was hell, but knowing that you're hurting and not knowing what to do—that's a different kind of torture."

Chelle reached out and took her mother's hand in hers. "There is something you could do. You could listen to a story and not judge me or Mason too harshly for it."

Over the next hour, she gave her parents a G-rated version of how she'd met Mason, how their engagement had come to be, and all the reasons she'd fallen in love with him. She told them about his journey and how Charles thought it might stop him from being able to love anyone. She ended her story by telling them how much she missed him and how she refused to believe she was wrong about him.

"So you were never actually engaged?" her father asked gruffly.

Chelle looked down at the diamond still on her finger. "I guess not, Dad."

Her mother gave her hand one final squeeze and suggested they all go to bed. Her father balked and started to say they should talk about what Chelle had shared.

Chelle's mother shook her head, encouraged her husband to join her at the door, and said, "Chelle doesn't need our advice; she needs that man of hers to call. And he will. Our daughter is no fool. Men, on the other hand, take the long way around what should be a short road."

Mason sat with his head in his hands in the private waiting room of a luxury rehab center in Malibu. He could hear the ocean waves crashing against the shore below, but they didn't soothe him. The last forty-eight hours had been hell, but if Ruby allowed herself to be admitted, it would be worth it.

Millie was a saint. By the time Mason had shown up, she'd already settled Ruby into bed and flushed every pill in her house down the toilet. She'd also arranged for a doctor to visit under a nondisclosure agreement to check that she hadn't taken more than the two pills she'd claimed to have taken.

Millie had left soon after Mason had arrived, but she returned a while later with a change of clothes for Mason and some toiletries. She didn't ask him about his relationship with Ruby, and he didn't offer her the history. She was—blissfully, thankfully—as professional as always.

When Ruby finally woke, she was embarrassed, then angry. She told him to leave several times, but he didn't. He told her he wasn't going anywhere until she agreed to check herself into rehab.

In an act of defiance, Ruby got shit-faced drunk on the alcohol neither he nor Millie had thought to dispose of. She flirted with him, yelled at him, then cried through most of the second night he was there. He held her and listened to her pour out her anguish until she fell asleep against him on the couch, and then he moved to sit in a chair across from her. When she woke the next morning, she met his eyes, and he knew she was ready.

He made arrangements for her stay at the very discreet beachside center and made sure they weren't followed by the press. The lack of paparazzi had been a relief in some ways, but in others it reaffirmed Ruby's reasons for feeling desperate. Interest in her was waning. Hopefully, her newest project would change that. She'd be fine as long as she was getting treatment.

One of the staff members came out to inform him that she was checked in and he could go. Mason stood and looked at the door Ruby had gone through. *Good luck. It's up to you now, Ruby.*

He turned his phone back on when he exited the building and listened to the messages from Millie. She'd moved around as many meetings as she could, but he had some the next day that were unavoidable. She also said there was a matter she didn't want to discuss over the phone, but it was important enough that he should drop into the office that day to see her.

He hadn't slept in two days and felt like shit, but if Millie said it was important, it was. He drove directly to his office.

As soon as Millie saw him she said, "You look like—"

"I know," he said tiredly. "Ruby's in, though, and that's what's important."

"She's lucky to have a friend like you."

In an uncharacteristic admission, Mason said, "I did it for me as much as for her."

"Well, you did good." She made a pained face. "I wish I didn't have bad news for you. This came in the mail today. It's a picture of you and Ruby leaving her house. It came with a nasty little note about how you deserve to be exposed for what you are, a man with no morals and no respect for women. I don't know who sent it, but it's already beginning to show up online."

She turned her computer so he could see his name in the headlines of a news blog. "Senator Thorne Leaves Small-Town Fiancée to Party with Ruby Skye. Next Governor? Not Anymore."

"That's gossip, not news," Mason snapped. He scanned the rest of the article. "Did any of the articles mention where I took Ruby today?"

Millie shook her head and turned her monitor back to its original position. "No, but this is damaging, Mason. That photo gave your opponents a human-interest story that paints you as a heartless bastard. You're losing voter support and fast."

"I don't care about the polls." Mason punched the wall with the side of his fist. If Chelle saw that photo, she'd be devastated. *Even when I'm doing something right, I'm fucking something up.*

"You need to. Ruby has been publicly intoxicated on several occasions lately. Linking your name with hers feeds into the image of you as someone who doesn't take anything seriously. Not your engagement. Not your seat in the state senate. Nothing. It undermines your water bill. I've had three senators call this morning to pull their support. It's not good. Is there any way you could do a press conference with Ms. Landon? Make up some reason you went to see Ruby? Maybe a stomach virus? If you can get Chelle to stand up and say that photo is a whole lot of nothing, the buzz surrounding it will die."

"I can't ask Chelle to do that. I won't bring her into this mess, and I swore I wouldn't tell anyone the truth about what I've been doing with Ruby. No. I'll handle this."

Millie folded her hands on her desktop. "What are you going to do?"

Chapter Eighteen

When Mason didn't call the first night, she told herself whatever emergency he'd needed to go back to deal with had likely kept him nonstop busy. That didn't stop her from lying awake all night waiting to hear from him, but it gave her some comfort as she fought back the doubt that was building within her.

Charles was wrong. Mason hadn't bolted. He'd gone back to deal with something.

Both Sarah and Melanie had called her the following day and tried to lure her out of her parents' home, but she didn't want to see either of them. She didn't want to hear their theories on why he hadn't found five minutes yet to call and tell her he'd made it back okay. Or tell her he missed her. Anything.

She helped her parents organize their tax papers, filed invoices they'd paid, and tried not to think about Mason. She knew what her mother would say if she asked her for advice. Mason would either call or he wouldn't; no amount of worrying over it would change that.

The second night without Mason was harder to handle than the first. She stopped checking her phone for texts, stopped picking it up every two minutes to make sure she hadn't missed a call. She included him in her prayers as she always did, but this time asked for the strength not to give up. She refused to believe she was wrong about him.

Yet when she thought back to the first night they'd met, she acknowledged he could say all the right things and not mean them. His false declaration of love for her had been a testament to his theatrical training. He could talk a weatherman into predicting sunshine on a rainy day. All he had to do was flash that Hollywood smile of his, and people wanted to believe him.

Was it wise to trust anything a man like that said?

Who am I kidding? He didn't say he loved me. He didn't ask me to wait for him.

He told me he didn't do relationships.

I didn't want to believe him.

Flashes of their time together came back to her as she lay, still dressed in jeans and a T-shirt, on her twin-size bed, missing him. From the way he'd introduced her to the pleasures of being with a man to how proud he'd looked when her father's damn horse hadn't killed him—there was not one moment of their time together Chelle regretted. Not one caress or one shared joke she would go back and change. Being with Mason had been like stepping into a fairy tale, albeit an X-rated one.

How do you give up on something like that?

A knock on her bedroom door startled her, and she sat up.

"Mind if we come in?" her mother asked, opening the door a few inches.

"That's fine," Chelle answered automatically. Her stomach did nervous flips when her father and mother both came to stand beside her bed. Her father had a piece of paper in one hand. It looked like a printout of a news article.

Oh my God. Chelle brought her hand to her mouth in horror. *Mason's dead.* She scooted to the edge of her bed and blinked back tears born from real fear. "What is it? What happened?"

"Your mother and I didn't know if we should show you this, but we decided it was better for you to hear it from us than someone in town."

Chelle clasped her hand over her heart. "Just say it."

Her father handed her the paper. Chelle took it and watched her mother move closer to hug her father. They both looked so concerned Chelle thought she might throw up. The first thing that jumped out on the page was Mason helping Ruby Skye into the backseat of a limo. It was the type of photo that looked as if it had been taken from the bushes without anyone being aware. Chelle read the headline twice and tried to read the article: "Senator Thorne Caught Ruby-Red-Handed." Her hands were shaking too much to allow her to read much more than the first paragraph, which accused Mason of returning to his wild partying days. They called him a liar. A cheat. Someone who had no respect for family values. "Is this really who you want representing you?" the article asked.

Mason had left her at their engagement party to meet up with his ex-girlfriend? She didn't want to believe it was true, but the evidence of where he'd been was right there in full color. She crumpled the paper in her hand and fought to breathe. *He could have told me. What happened to not wanting to hurt me?*

Her mother sat beside her on the bed and rubbed her back, soothing her as she'd always done. "I'm so sorry, Chelle. I didn't want to believe it when I first saw it, but it's all over the news."

Her father didn't say anything, and for that, Chelle was grateful. She knew what he was thinking, but if he'd said it, she probably would have broken down in tears.

Chelle threw the paper on the floor. *It* was *too good to be true.* She cleared her throat and took a deep breath. "At least now I know why he's not calling."

"Oh, honey," her mother cooed.

Chelle blinked back tears she refused to shed. "I'll be okay. The whole thing was wrong from the start. Who gets engaged and then tries to date? My mistake was forgetting it wasn't real."

Her father made an angry growling noise, then walked out of the room. Her mother stayed and continued to rub Chelle's back. "It didn't look like a mistake when I saw you with him. If he really did run back to California to party with that . . . that woman, then he's the one who made a mistake, and it's one he'll probably spend the rest of his life regretting."

Chelle sniffed. "If? Mom, that photo is pretty damning."

Her mother bent, picked the paper off the floor, and smoothed it over her lap. She studied the photo. "I stared at this photo long and hard before we brought it in to show you. I don't care what the article says. Everyone knows you can't believe half of what is in the news. There's no denying he left you to go to her, but he's not happy about it. He doesn't look like a man who just spent a wild night with that woman. He's miserable. And sad. Take a look for yourself."

Chelle glanced over and said coldly, "Or hungover."

"Maybe," her mother said gently and laid the paper down on the bed beside her.

"Mom, he hasn't called me. Not once. Not a text. Not an e-mail. Nothing. It's time for me to admit I am not as good a judge of character as I like to imagine I am."

Smoothing her hands down the front of her jeans, her mother said, "Let yourself cry it out tonight, baby. But tomorrow morning you get up nice and early, and you go for a trail ride with your dad and me. Then we'll come back, have a nice lunch, and decide where you want to fly off to next."

That did bring tears to Chelle's eyes. "Don't you think I've made enough of a mess of everything already? Maybe it's better if I just stay here and work on the ranch like we talked about."

Her mother put a hand beneath her chin and turned her face so their eyes met. "Chelle Susan Landon, you will do no such thing. You think Mason is the only man out there? He's not. He's also not the reason you wanted to leave here. Your dad and I know you don't want the same life we've had. We don't need you to be a carbon copy of us. What matters is that you're happy. Where are your cards with destinations on them? Pick another. You went riding into the wind, baby, and you fell off. What did I always tell you about that?"

Tears were streaming down Chelle's cheeks, but they were the result of a complicated mix of feelings. There were some things she knew she needed to let go of, and other things she was so grateful would always be there. "How did you get so wise, Mom?"

After a final hug, her mother stood. "I guess it's because I had a wonderful mother who understood that I fell in love with a diamond in the rough. Your father came back from Vietnam an angry man. It took time and patience to work through that. She made sure I knew the difference between being someone's doormat and being someone's rock. I love your father and the life we've made together, but I could survive if he left me. That's what I want for you, Chelle. Don't be afraid to love with all your heart, but know that no matter what happens, it doesn't change who you are."

Her mother closed the door behind her. Chelle lay back down without turning off the light. She spent a good amount of time staring at the photo of Mason and Ruby before she eventually conceded that the answers she sought couldn't be found there. *Why don't you call, Mason? Even if it's just to tell me it's over?* She rummaged beside her bed for the present Sarah and Melanie had given her. She closed her eyes, reached inside, and pulled out a card.

Niagara Falls. *At least my tears won't show there.*

She fell asleep with the article and the card tucked beneath her pillow.

The next morning, Chelle woke to the sound of her cell phone ringing. The sun was streaming through the window, evidence she'd slept later than she normally did. The caller had a California area code. Chelle sat straight up in her bed and answered in a rush. "Mason?"

"Am I speaking with Chelle Landon?" a woman asked in a businesslike tone.

"Yes," Chelle answered, rubbing the sleep out of her eyes.

"I'm Millie Capri, Senator Thorne's administrative assistant."

Oh my God. He wouldn't have his secretary tell me it's over, would he? "What can I do for you, Mrs. Capri?"

"Senator Thorne is giving a statement to the press at four o'clock this afternoon. It would be a huge benefit to him if you were there by his side."

Chelle shook her head in disbelief. "Are you serious? Or is this some kind of joke?"

"Considering the negative attention the press has given him regarding his association with Ruby Skye, your presence would go a long way in diffusing the rumor that he's cheating on you."

Chelle's breath caught in her throat. "Are you saying he's not?"

"I can neither confirm nor deny what Senator Thorne does in his personal life, but I can tell you the rumor may cost him not only the passing of the bill he's been working on, but also his run for governor."

Chelle's temper began to rise. "Give me one good reason why I should care about either."

Mason's secretary fell silent for a moment, then said, "If you love him, get your ass on a flight out here. He needs you." She cleared her throat and in a professional voice said, "I can make the flight arrangements if you'd like."

Chelle held the phone away from her before bringing it back to her ear. She didn't know whether to laugh or cry. "If Mason wants me out there, he can ask me himself."

In a no-nonsense tone, Mrs. Capri said, "He won't, and he doesn't know I made this call. I'll text you the information you'll need when you arrive. This number is my private cell. If you need anything, don't hesitate to contact me."

The line went dead.

She dug the photo of Mason and Ruby out from under her pillow and frowned down at it before waving it at the powers above. *Is this a test? What am I supposed to do with this?*

Mason was sitting in his office, answering e-mails and phone calls. He was winning back support for his bill, but it was slow going—one excruciating negotiation at a time. He had to prove to his colleagues that voters would not see supporting the protection of the state's water supply as an endorsement of the lascivious lifestyle he had reportedly ditched his small-town fiancée for.

He hung up the phone on his desk and left his hand on the receiver. He'd almost called Chelle once or twice—okay, maybe a hundred times—so far that day. He'd even started dialing her number once, then slammed the phone down. There was nothing to say, not yet.

If he called her and somehow convinced her he'd been with Ruby for reasons other than what was in the news, what then? She'd want to come to Sacramento to be with him, and he wouldn't put her through the media storm that was swirling around him. Right now, he was being vilified while Chelle was a martyr people were proclaiming public sympathy for.

That could change in a flash.

The paparazzi loved to build people up only to tear them down. He wouldn't let that happen to Chelle. He'd promised her that when they eventually did break up, he would do it in a way that would show her in a good light.

Well, he'd certainly done that. Photos of Chelle in Fort Mavis were popping up in the media. She was the poster child for good old-fashioned values. California was a progressive state, but even its citizens didn't like the idea of a governor who spat on core American values like honesty and family.

Mason moved his hand to rub his tired eyes. The kindest thing he could do for Chelle would be to keep her as far removed from that insanity as possible.

His cell phone rang in his pocket. It was Charles. Mason let it ring through to his voice mail. He really didn't want to hear Charles gloat about being right. Nor did he want to defend how he'd left or why he hadn't called Chelle.

Mason had faced worse alone, and he knew he would survive this, too. At the end of the day, he wasn't a hero; he was a survivor. Nothing less. Nothing more.

Chelle was better off without him.

Chapter Nineteen

Chelle had changed her mind at least three times by the time she finished showering and doing her hair. She reached for a pair of jeans, then stopped. *If I'm doing this, I need to look the part.* She dug through her closet for a simple dress and matching shoes. Conservative, yet attractive. When she met her eyes in the mirror, she thought about what her mother had said the night before. *I am not afraid to love with my whole heart, because no matter what happens in California, it won't change me.*

Before heading downstairs to talk to her parents, she reached for her cell phone to make a call. It rang three times, then Charles answered. "Chelle? Is everything all right?"

Chelle took a deep breath before saying, "At four o'clock Mason is making a statement to the press regarding the photo with Ruby Skye. I want to be there to support him. I know you have a private plane. Will you fly me out there? There isn't much time to decide, so I need your decision now."

"Did you speak to him?"

Chelle closed her eyes, bit her bottom lip, then said firmly, "I didn't need to. I trust him, and if he went to see Ruby, there was a reason. I'm not going to embarrass him. If I get there and he doesn't want me at his side, I'll come home. No one will know I was even there. But he's under attack right now, and he needs all the support he can get. I want to show him he's not alone." She paused before plowing on. "You should come with me. He could use a friend by his side right about now."

"We'll fly out of the small airfield south of town in an hour," Charles said, then asked abruptly, "Do you need me to send a car for you?"

"No, I can get a ride. One more thing."

"Yes?"

"How many people can fit in your plane?"

About five hours later at a small private airport, Chelle met Mrs. "Please, call me Millie" Capri for the first time. Chelle introduced her to her parents, Sarah, Tony, Charles, and Melanie.

"How much time do we have?" Charles asked in a demanding tone that made most people jump nervously. "Can you guarantee Chelle won't be seen?"

Millie didn't flinch. "I could move the president of the United States in and out of the building without the press being aware; I'm confident we can sneak all of you in without being detected."

Chelle's father had agreed to come, but he wasn't yet sold on the endeavor. "I don't understand why we couldn't call him to tell him we were coming."

"Senator Thorne would have said it's not necessary," answered Millie.

"Are we sure it is?" Roger growled the question.

His wife took his hand in hers. "It is to Chelle."

Chelle went to stand in front of her father. The closer they came to seeing Mason, the more anxious she became. It was too easy to start worrying about what his response would be to seeing her. What if he turned her away? What if he actually had chosen Ruby over her? She refused to let her fears win. "Remember what I said, Dad. This is about showing him we care, not pushing our way up there with him. He may not want us next to him when he gives his statement."

"If I came all this way and he doesn't want us here, I'll give the press something else to write about."

Chelle shook her head frantically. "Don't, Dad. Please don't make things worse."

With a frustrated sigh, her father agreed.

Millie led them to a line of cars with tinted windows.

Sarah said, "This is kind of exciting, isn't it?" When no one agreed with her, she added, "Say what you want, but when we all look back at this later, this is going to be one of the coolest things we've done."

Melanie winked at Sarah's husband. "If you can, you should probably keep her quiet in front of the cameras."

Tony shrugged and smiled at his wife. Chelle wasn't sure if that meant that he wouldn't or that he would try, but Sarah would do what she pleased anyway.

The ride to the statehouse felt endless. Chelle knew she was doing the right thing, but her nerves were frayed, and her emotions were all over the place. She was pretty sure her parents had agreed to come simply because they didn't want her to be alone if this went wrong.

Charles's support seemed genuine. Melanie was there both for her fiancé and as moral support for Chelle. Sarah was thrilled to have been invited to watch what she was positive would be the day her brother's best friend realized how much he loved Chelle.

When they arrived at the statehouse, Millie had the cars pull down a back alley that led to an entrance blocked off from the press. Plainclothes security men were scattered about, watching for anyone who shouldn't have been in that area.

One of them opened the door to the building. Chelle hesitated before walking through it. She turned to Millie. "I'm not wrong, am I?"

"We'll soon find out," Millie answered and ushered her inside. She gave them all instructions to stay in the hallway she led them to. She pointed to a door at the end of the hallway. "Senator Thorne will enter through that door in about ten minutes." She pointed to a second door on the other end of the hall. "The press is on the other side of that door. I'll be in the back of the conference room. If I don't see you walk out with him, I'll have the cars readied to take you back to your plane. Remember, this is a press statement. You're not to answer anyone's questions. Let Senator Thorne say what he needs to say, and that's it."

Barely able to breathe, Chelle said, "Thank you, Mrs. Capri."

Millie smiled. "I told you, call me Millie. I hope this works out. Mason needs someone like you in his life. You did good, Chelle." She looked at Charles, then back at Chelle. "You did real good." She looked down at her watch and said, "Five minutes. Good luck." Then she left the hall through a door that led to the back of the conference room.

.

Mason adjusted his tie in the mirror and practiced his winning smile. He looked and felt like shit. *That's what three days without sleep will do.*

He gave himself a mental shake and focused on rehearsing his statement. Rather than read a speech, he had points he intended to address. First, he would make it clear he wasn't taking questions. Second, he would announce his breakup with Chelle and claim responsibility. He'd make a quick joke about discovering he wasn't marriage material, then lead into how little relevance that had when it came to the current drought in California or unemployment numbers. If he handled it correctly, he'd sway the press back to his side. He'd done it before.

His biggest regret was that Chelle would hear about their breakup via his public statement. He took out his phone and called her. He hadn't rehearsed what he would say to her, but he knew he had to say something. She picked up on the first ring. "Chelle, it's Mason."

"I know," she said softly.

"There's something I need to tell you."

"Mason, whatever you have to say to me, you should say in person."

She's right, but there's no time now. "I would if there were time. I was wrong to avoid having this conversation, but I'm just about to speak to the press, and I want you to be prepared for what I'll say."

"Mason, I'm at the statehouse. I'm in the hallway leading to the conference room. If you want to tell me something, you know where to find me." With that, she hung up.

Mason tore out of his office. He wouldn't believe she was there until he saw her with his own eyes. He hadn't given her any reason to believe in him. In fact, he wouldn't have blamed her if she'd refused to even speak to him. The photo of him with Ruby had been damning enough to sway public opinion against him. Why would she come to him now?

He didn't wait for the elevator. He sprinted down the stairs and ripped open the door to the hallway where she'd said she was. He couldn't breathe as he searched the hall for her. He recognized the other people there, but during that first moment, they didn't matter. There she was, exactly as she'd said she would be. Waiting for him.

Every disappointment he'd ever endured, every wall he'd constructed around his heart fell away as he walked toward her. In that moment, he felt lighter, freer and was tempted to run to her. She met him in the middle of the hallway. Before they said a word to each other, they kissed passionately.

Emotions that had long been locked within Mason burst out and temporarily overwhelmed him. He broke off the kiss and simply held her to his chest. "What are you doing here, Chelle?" he asked huskily.

She tipped her head back and touched the wetness on one of his cheeks in awe. "Are you crying?"

He hid his face in her hair, hugged her tighter, and blinked a few times quickly. He didn't care what others might think of his emotional display. All that mattered was that she had come to him and how good it felt to hold her again. "I should have called you. I wanted to. I don't know why I didn't."

She gave him a smile full of such love his eyes misted up again. "We can talk about that later. Right now, all that matters is that we're here for you. All of us."

Mason raised his head and looked around the hall. Chelle's parents were there, along with Charles, Melanie, Sarah, and Tony. "You're all here for the press statement?"

Chelle nodded and stepped back. "More would have come if Charles's plane had been bigger. We're here to stand beside you while you defend yourself, or cheer you on from the back of the room, or wait for you here. Tell us what you need."

Mason looked around again and ran a hand through his hair. He gazed down at Chelle. "You're not angry with me?"

She raised her eyebrows. "Oh, I'm furious. You hurt me, Mason. You really did. We are far from okay right now. But where I come from, even when we have our differences, if trouble comes for one of us, it's handled by all of us. You're not alone, Mason. Not unless you want to be."

Charles nodded his agreement from behind Chelle. Chelle's mother wiped tears from her eyes. Sarah and Melanie were in similar states. Tony watched without saying anything, which from Mason's experience was a sign of support in itself. Chelle's father appeared less than happy about being there, but Mason couldn't blame him for that. Mason had hurt his daughter.

Millie reentered the hallway and approached Mason and Chelle. "Senator Thorne, the press is getting antsy out there. Are you ready?"

Mason frowned at his assistant and asked, "Did you arrange this?"

Without batting an eyelash, Millie answered, "I told your fiancée if she cared about you, she'd better get her ass on a plane and get here. I didn't say more than that."

Mason stepped away from Chelle and gave Millie a hug so tight it had her laughing and gasping for air. "You are amazing."

Millie backed away, adjusted her hair, and returned to her usual unflappable self. "How would you like to do this?"

Mason addressed the group as a whole. "I don't know what to say. None of you should have to be here today. The press can be unpredictably ugly. I didn't mean for any of you to get caught up in this."

Chelle slid under his arm and hugged his side. "The only question you need to answer is if you want us here."

He met her eyes, and for a moment the world disappeared around them. "More than anything I've ever wanted in my whole life." He kissed her gently, then turned back to everyone else. "I can't control how the press will spin this, but if you'd like to stand behind me while I make my statement, I'd be grateful to have you there."

One by one everyone showed their agreement by either a nod or a word or two. With his heart thudding loudly in his chest, Mason said, "Then let's do this."

Mason walked out to the podium holding Chelle's hand and waving for the others to follow. Chelle stood beside him while the others stayed behind, off to one side but in view of the reporters. Mason crumpled up his initial speaking points and said, "I am not a perfect man. You don't have to dig deeply if you want to find dirt on me. Hold your questions today. I am not here to defend or explain myself. My opposition can try to muddy the waters with photos and lies, but voters are smart enough to see through that. I am here to respectfully request that we turn our attention away from my personal life and back to the very real issues facing our state. We need to ensure that our coastlines are protected, that we have enough water to support our population, and that we don't allow corporations to bully us into legislature that lines their pockets instead of ensuring our future. Let's work together to solve these issues." He flashed the press his most charming smile and added, "And if you're real nice, some of you may get invited to our wedding."

Just like that, the tide turned again. Several of the reporters called out questions about when the wedding would be. One called out, "Is that the Takedown Cowgirl? Can we get a photo of her with Mr. Dery?" Mason guided Chelle away from the podium without responding to the questions.

Once outside the conference room, Chelle shook her head in amazement. "That's it? That's all it took to get them to forget about the photo?"

Mason cupped her face with his hand. "You have to understand the nature of the beast. They need a story. They don't care what it is."

Millie was beside the group again and said, "I've taken the liberty of securing a few suites for the night at the Grand City Hotel. If you're ready, the cars are outside and will take you there now."

As they walked toward the cars together, Mason pulled Chelle close to his side. He lagged behind the rest so he and Chelle could have a moment alone. "We need to talk."

She spun around to face him. "What you need to do is apologize. And then I need to somehow believe you'll never do it again. I don't know what happened out here, but there was no reason you couldn't have called me, even if it was just to say you had nothing to say. That's not the way to treat someone you say you care about."

Her reprimand rocked him back onto his heels. "You're right."

His quick agreement seemed to confuse her. "I know I am."

"Would it help if I said when I saw you in the hallway, I knew I'd been a fool? I love you. I was afraid to let myself see it, but I can't imagine a day of my life without you in it. I've been considering running for governor, but I can make my life wherever you are. I've never had anyone stand with me the way you and your family did. I don't know how to thank you except to promise that I will spend the rest of my life showing you how much I love you."

Chelle raised a hand and placed two fingers on Mason's mouth to silence him. "If this is a proposal, I can't accept it."

Mason's mood plummeted, and his gut twisted painfully. He took her hand in his. "I hurt you. I understand it'll take you time to forgive me, but I'll ask you every day if that's what it takes to get you to agree to marry me for real."

A funny expression passed over Chelle's face. "My dad and I made a deal when I told him I was coming here. I will not accept any proposal from you unless he gives us his blessing. He'll want to talk to you tonight."

Mason's gaze flew to where Chelle's father was standing, waiting for them. He didn't doubt he could persuade Chelle to defy her father, but he didn't want to.

This time, he was doing it the Fort Mavis way.

Chapter Twenty

After one of the most awkward dinners he'd ever attended, Mason asked Chelle's father if he could speak to him, and the two walked away from the group so they could talk in private. Mason was used to knowing what to say, but he didn't normally care so much about the outcome of a conversation. He wanted to choose his words perfectly. "Roger."

"Mr. Landon for now."

Okay. "Mr. Landon, I love your daughter."

"I'm listening."

"I want to marry her."

"I guessed that much already from your display at the statehouse."

Mason cleared his throat. "I'm asking for your blessing."

Chelle's father rubbed his chin in thought. "Mr. Thorne, I want you to put yourself in my position for a moment. You talked my daughter into some crazy fake engagement you both took as far as two people could take that lie. You let us have a public celebration for something you knew wasn't true and then embarrassed my daughter in front of the entire nation. You hurt her. And you disappointed those of us who took you at face value. She might have forgiven you, but I'm not as quick to. Why should I believe you're good enough for my daughter?"

Mason squared his shoulders. "I don't know what to say besides I love her. I'm sorry I lied to you and to everyone in your town. I didn't mean for it to go as far as it did. And I certainly never meant to hurt Chelle. I regret that the most. I know I haven't lived a spotless life so far, but I'm a different man when I'm with your daughter. She makes me want to be a better man."

"Prove it."

"Excuse me?"

"You're a man who uses fancy words and talks his way out of trouble a bit too easily. Words mean nothing to me, son. You want me to believe you love my daughter, show me."

"How exactly am I supposed to do that?"

"We're all heading home tomorrow morning. Chelle is coming with us. You want to prove you love my daughter? Bring your father to the ranch to meet us."

"I haven't talked to my father in over ten years."

"Then it should be a mighty interesting visit."

Mason fisted his hand. "It's never going to happen. Ask me to do anything else. I'll do it. But not that."

Roger folded his arms across his chest in a move that vaguely reminded him of a stance Chelle would have taken. He said, "Son, you've got a lot to learn about love. You think it's all passion and excitement? That is only a small piece. Real love requires strength of character and courage. I'm not yet sure you have either. Go find your father. Bring him to Fort Mavis. Show me I'm wrong about you."

Mason went for a long walk after speaking to Chelle's father. He was angry at first. He shouldn't have to prove himself to anyone. Then he thought about how Chelle had come to him—in the face of damning rumors and his seeming desertion.

Chelle had what her father referred to as strength of character and courage. He wanted to be a man who deserved that kind of woman.

He was leaning on a wall outside the hotel when Chelle found him. She met his eyes, then blushed. "My parents asked me to sleep in their suite tonight. I didn't feel like I could say no."

Mason pulled her against him and looped his arms around her waist. "It's no longer shocking you stayed a virgin until twenty-five."

Chelle swatted at his shoulder. "You love it."

He growled and kissed her neck. "I do. And I love you."

Chelle pulled his head up and studied his face. "I love you, too. I'm still angry with you, though."

"I know. I spoke to your father. He said you're all going back to Fort Mavis tomorrow."

"I hope you understand why I have to," Chelle said. "Part of me wants to stay with you, but I can't when all I'd be thinking about is if you'd leave me again. Trust is a funny thing, Mason. It's as fragile as it is important. I want to believe you love me. I want that more than you know, but . . ."

Mason exhaled slowly. "You need me to show you."

Chelle tensed. "I guess I do."

He kissed her lightly. "Your father wants me to do something before he'll give us his blessing."

Chelle let out a shaky breath. "Did it involve castration?"

"No, thankfully," Mason said with a slight laugh, then gripped her hips. "Your father wants to meet mine. He asked me to bring him to your ranch. My father may not even want to talk to me, but I know where he lives, and I suppose it's time for me to face my past."

Chelle hugged him tighter. "Do you want me to go with you?"

"I want to say yes, but my father and I have some things to say to each other, and that won't happen if you're there." Chelle's acceptance humbled him. He didn't know what he had ever done to deserve to be loved by such a kind woman, but he swore he would spend the rest of his life earning that love. He kissed her soundly, then said, "Which doesn't mean I don't want you with me. Chelle, I want to explain about Ruby."

Her heart was in her eyes as she answered, "You don't have to."

"Yes, I do." He knew in that moment that no matter what happened between them, Chelle would never betray Ruby or him. "There are things you don't know about me, but you need to." He told her about how much his life had fallen apart after his mother's death. He described his relationship with Ruby and didn't gloss over how mutually destructive it had been. By the time he repeated what Ruby had said to him the night of their engagement party, Chelle was wiping tears from her cheeks. "I promised Ruby I would never say what I did for her, but I couldn't not be there for her. I know that place all too well. I couldn't leave her before I was sure she was going to get help. That doesn't mean I still have feelings for her. I hope you understand that."

Chelle wiped both of her cheeks with her hands and sniffed. "You make it impossible to stay angry with you."

"I don't want you to forgive me. Not yet. I want to earn your trust." Mason rested his chin on her forehead. "That's why I'm going to speak to my father. You see something in me that I want to see, too."

Two days later, Mason parked his car in the driveway of a modest home in the suburbs of Elk Grove, a far cry from the mansion his parents had purchased with the money from Mason's first blockbuster movie.

Mason was halfway up the steps of the house when the door opened. Hearing his father's voice on the phone when they'd made arrangements to meet up had felt surreal, but seeing him standing in the doorway brought the past crashing back. It felt as if only a day had passed since he'd gotten the call announcing his mother's death. His memories of how little his father had said to him during and after that time were vividly painful.

He forced himself to walk up the rest of the steps. He wasn't sure what he expected to feel for his father, but at first, outside of anger, there was nothing. Absolutely nothing. Chelle's father could meet Jarrett Thorne if he wanted to, but if he was hoping to witness a touching father-son reunion, he'd be disappointed.

"Mason, it's good to see you."

His father looked very different from the man he remembered. He was older, but that wasn't all it was. The father he'd known had always worn specially tailored clothing and had his hair cut in the latest style. This man was in jeans and a T-shirt. He looked . . . normal. Mason could imagine him donning a suit for a nine-to-five job, then spending his weekends mowing his own lawn. It was further evidence of how little of a bond there was between them. The father Mason had known was nonexistent in the man before him. "Thank you for seeing me on such short notice."

Jarrett opened the door wider. "Come on in. Pardon the mess. Emmett and Austin are in an after-school club. Every creation they come home with is precious, at least that's what they'll tell you. Cristy should be back with them shortly."

Mason wanted to be gone before then, but he didn't say so. He followed his father into the house and then the living room. It was furnished tastefully, but definitely with comfort in mind more than fashion. Mason took a seat in a chair, and his father sat across from him.

The silence rested between them long and heavy before Jarrett said, "I still can't believe you're a senator, but I always did say you could do anything you set your mind to."

"I'm not here to discuss my career. I also don't need you to pretend you give a shit about how I've been."

Mason's father leaned back in his chair with a sad, resigned expression on his face. "Then why are you here?"

Mason let go of the last shred of hope he'd had that there was anything left between him and his father. "I'm getting married."

Jarrett smiled. "I know; it's all over the news."

Mason didn't smile back. "Her father wants to meet you. I realize it's a lot to ask, but I'd appreciate it if you flew down there to have dinner with him. I'd pay for the trip, of course."

Jarrett gave Mason a long, measured look. "I can afford the flight. When would you like me to go?"

Mason's eyes flew to his father's. He hadn't expected him to agree so easily. "Friday night would probably work best for everyone."

"All I need is a time and address, and I'll be there."

Mason gave him both, then stood. "Thank you."

Jarrett moved to stand next to him. "That's all you came for?"

"Yes," Mason answered shortly. "What else is there?"

To Mason's surprise, his father's eyes shone with emotion. "I was hoping you came to talk."

Mason shrugged. "Whatever we had to say stopped being important a long time ago."

His father blinked quickly and sat on one of the arms of a couch. "It doesn't have to be that way, Mason."

Mason waved an angry hand in the air. "Don't you dare make it sound like what happened between us was my choice. My life went to shit after Mom died, and where were you? Did you pick up the phone once to see if I was okay? No. You didn't. So you'll have to excuse me for not believing this whole fatherly act."

Jarrett rubbed a hand over his face. "I couldn't imagine you'd want to hear from me. I didn't have anything to offer you. Your mother loved to spend money, and we went through much more than we had. I couldn't hate you for not wanting me as your manager anymore; it had stopped being healthy for any of us. After your mother died, I was in bad shape for about a year. Not just financially. Her death made me see who we'd become, who we'd made you into, and I was ashamed. I drank myself nearly to death. Is that a man you would have wanted to call you?"

"It doesn't matter anymore," Mason said.

His father's face went white with emotion. "I didn't know how to be a father to you, Mason. You were a star from the day you were born. I chased the fame and money, failed you and your mother, and I have to live with that knowledge every day of my life. But Cristy helped me see that beating myself up over it wasn't undoing what I had done. My death wouldn't have brought your mother back." He reached out a hand toward Mason, then let it drop. "I wasn't a good husband or father the first time around, but I've had a second chance to get it right, and I can look at myself in the mirror now without reaching for a bottle of Jack. I know I should have called you. But I didn't think you'd want to hear from me."

Mason was at a loss for how to respond to his father's raw, emotional display of regret. "How old are your sons?"

His father smiled with a flicker of sadness. "They're both seven. Emmett was born four minutes before Austin and takes his role of big brother very seriously. They're not identical. Emmett looks more like Cristy's side of the family than mine. He has her eyes and often her expressions. Austin reminds me of you. He's going to be a heartbreaker when he's older. Girls already fawn all over him." Jarrett stood. "I won't make the same mistake with him that I made with you, Mason. I don't have a career path chosen for him. Both of them will have normal childhoods. We should have let you have the same."

A long awkward moment passed. Mason motioned toward the door. "Text me about Friday and your flight."

"Are you sure you can't stay a little longer? Emmett and Austin were hoping to meet you."

"Another time," Mason said. Seeing his father again had been enough for one day. He hadn't known what to expect and was somewhat relieved that it had gone better than expected, but he was realistic enough to keep his expectations low. He had done what he came for. More than that was just asking for trouble. He walked out of the house the way he had come in. His father followed, then stood at the top of the steps watching Mason walk around to the driver's side of his car. Mason opened the door but paused before getting in. "This is important to me."

"I'll be there."

Mason nodded, slid into his car, and peeled out of the driveway, eager to put distance between himself and his past. On the way to his apartment, he called Chelle.

"How did it go?" she asked in a rush.

"Tell your parents my father will be there Friday."

"Really?"

"Really."

"So it went well?"

Mason cut in and out of traffic, grinding the gears of his car as he took out some of his frustrations on his vehicle. "Define *well*. I saw him. We spoke. I asked him to fly down to meet your parents, and he agreed to. That's it, really. Honestly, I couldn't get out of there fast enough."

"That can't be all that happened. He must have said something."

"He tried to justify the last ten years. I understand now what your father meant when he said words mean nothing to him. All he wanted to talk about was how he's going to do better with his new sons. It meant nothing to me."

"He has children? You didn't tell me that."

"I didn't know about them until recently. I haven't exactly kept up with my father's life."

"Are they his biologically?"

"Yes."

"I've always wished I weren't an only child, but my mother couldn't have any after me. You have brothers, Mason." Chelle sounded a hell of a lot more excited about it than he did.

"Half brothers."

She made a little sound, and he could picture the exact expression she'd have on her face as she made it. *God, I miss her.*

"How old are they?"

"His kids?"

"Your brothers."

"He said they're seven."

"Did you meet them?"

"No. I didn't see a reason to. It's very unlikely I'll even see my father again after this week."

"Why?"

"What do you mean, 'Why?'"

"Why wouldn't you see him again?"

"Chelle, my family isn't close like yours." He gave Chelle a quick summary of what his father had said his life had been like before and after his mother had died. "My father cares about his new wife and kids, not me. I've made peace with that."

"Have you, Mason? What happened was awful. You lost both of your parents when your mother died. My grandfather used to say we are the best and worst of everything we've been through, but the art of living is taking that and making something good out of it. Your father didn't believe you could love him, so he turned his back on you. You don't believe he can love you, so you're doing the same to him and your brothers. When does it end? And how long will it be before you decide I can't love you and you do the same to me?"

"That would never happen." Mason pulled off the highway into a rest area. He gripped the steering wheel.

"It might if you choose to run from this instead of face it. Mason, my father doesn't care about actually meeting your father. He wanted you to go see him. There is nothing more important to my father than family, and honestly, I feel the same way. I want to build a life with you, but I'll admit it scares me when I see you shutting people out. What are you going to do when I disappoint you one day? I will. There isn't a single perfect person on the planet, Mason. Not me. Not you. Will you stay and work it out? I need to know you will. Otherwise, why marry at all?"

"I would fight for us, Chelle. You have to know that."

There was resolve in her gently spoken request. "Then show me. Go meet your brothers, Mason. Find it in your heart to forgive your father. Not for him—for us. It doesn't matter if they're the good people we hope they are; it matters that you can open your heart enough to show them you are."

"That's quite an ultimatum, Chelle."

"I'm worth it," Chelle said with her usual surety and hung up.

Mason pulled his car back onto the highway and headed to his apartment. He didn't get angry with Chelle the way he had when her father had said something similar to him. Chelle loved him. She was the one person in the world he was 100 percent certain of. He wanted her to feel the same certainty when it came to him. Before he went to bed that night, he called his father and asked if he could visit again the next day. "I'd like to meet Emmett and Austin if they'd still like to meet me."

His father said, "We'll be here." Although his answer was brief, his tone revealed that he was happier about it than Mason had expected.

Mason spent the night thinking about what Chelle had said. Could he face the past without becoming the person he'd been back then? As soon as he asked himself that question, he realized he'd hung on to the fears of a young man well past when he should have.

He wasn't eighteen and alone. He was a successful man with a loving fiancée, and friends who had shown their loyalty to him. Chelle was right; it was time to forgive—but not just his father. Sometime around midnight Mason realized he was still angry with his mother for leaving the way she had and with himself for falling apart when it happened. He didn't need to talk through each revelation with his father; he needed to let the anger go.

Very late that night Mason called Chelle. Her voice was groggy from sleep. "Mason? Is everything all right?"

"I love you, Chelle, and I'm going to spend the rest of my life showing you."

"It's two a.m.," she said adorably, still half asleep. "But I love you, too. Is that all you called for?"

"I'm going to see my father again later today, and this time I asked to see my brothers."

Her voice was warm and pleased. "Mason, that's wonderful."

"I wish I were there with you."

"Me too. Are you still coming on Friday?"

"Yes, but I have a question. How would your father feel about more company? They may not want to go, but if things work out tomorrow, I'd like to ask all of them to come along."

"Mason Thorne, do you have any idea how much I love you?"

He smiled and rolled onto his back on his bed, picturing her naked beside him. "No, but I have ideas about how you can show me."

"Show you, huh?"

"Isn't that how this works?" He was only teasing her, but it was too much fun not to. "I show you, and then you show me?"

"I'm hanging up now, Mason," she said, laughing before she ended the call.

Mason threw the phone on the bed next to him and smiled.

Later that day, Mason arrived at his father's house while his brothers were still at school. They talked about nothing in particular, but the conversation felt better than yesterday's. He didn't have to—and didn't want to—rehash everything that had happened between them. He wanted to move on, and that's what they were doing.

The door of the house burst open, and two young boys ran directly into the living room and came to a halt in front of Mason. They stood before him, looking him over, before one of them said, "He's old."

The other was kinder. "Not as old as Mr. Kensley."

A beautiful blonde woman in her early fifties entered the room behind them, looking a bit flushed. "Austin and Emmett, didn't I tell you to bring in your bags from the car?"

The taller of the two defended his decision. "We were afraid Mason would leave again."

The other boy, who was just a hair shorter, rounded his big blue eyes and flashed his mother a smile that would melt any woman's heart. "Can we get them later, Mom? Please?"

Oh, he's good, Mason thought. *Too good.*

Cristy ruffled their hair and sighed. "I guess. It's not every day you meet your brother."

Brother. It wasn't until he heard the term while the boys were in front of him that he felt the full impact of who they were. He had brothers. Two young boys who were looking at him expectantly without anger or resentment.

Chelle had once said to him, "You're not alone, Mason. Not unless you want to be." Mason looked at his father and his new family, and the sight filled him with hope. If he was the best and worst of who his father was, then he could start fresh and succeed just as his father had. He could have a simpler life, one where family and friends replaced drugs and partying.

Jarrett stood between his oldest and youngest children and said, "Mason, this is Emmett and this is Austin. Boys, this is Mason, my oldest son."

Emmett looked him over critically. "I saw a few of your movies. You could totally tell the spaceships weren't real."

Mason smiled. "At the time, those special effects were considered cutting-edge."

Emmett held his gaze. "Dad says you live in Sacramento."

"I do," Mason answered. He could see the wheels in his brother's head turning and anticipated the next question.

"Why have you never been here?"

Mason looked up at his father, then at a concerned Cristy. She rushed to say, "Emmett, now isn't the time to ask a question like that. Mason is here now."

"It's a valid question," Mason said and crouched down so he was eye to eye with Emmett. "I've never had a brother, so I suppose I didn't know how to be one."

Austin leapt forward enthusiastically. "It's easy." He tackled his twin to the floor. "All you have to do is grab Em like this, toss him down like that, and sit on him." Austin sat on the middle of his brother's back with a huge smile.

Jarrett rolled his eyes. "Austin, don't sit on Emmett."

"He likes it," Austin claimed and bounced on him.

"I do not," Emmett said loudly. "Get off me."

"Make me," Austin jeered.

Emmett spun around beneath him and skillfully whipped Austin under him, then pinned him to the floor. A vase on one of the side tables teetered, but Cristy steadied it. "Off the floor, now."

Emmett bounced on Austin. "He started it."

"We've talked about wrestling in the house," said Cristy. "I'm going to count to three, and if I don't have two well-behaved sons standing beside me, no one is watching TV for a week."

Emmett stood and offered his hand to his brother to help him up. Austin took it, and in a heartbeat, they were back to being buddies again.

Jarrett looked at his suddenly angelic young sons and said, "We put them in karate because we thought it would stop them from fighting, but now they just do it with more finesse."

Mason chuckled. "I can see that."

"Would you like to stay for dinner, Mason?" Cristy asked. "We'd love to have you."

Mason's first impulse was to say no, but both of his younger brothers froze and waited for his answer. He could walk away from them. There was no law saying he had to have a relationship with them, but Mason knew too well how it felt to be rejected. Back then, it hadn't mattered how many fans adored him if he didn't have his father's approval. "I'd like that, Cristy. Thank you."

His father walked over and put a hand on his shoulder. "You don't know how much this means to me."

Mason let go of the rest of his anger. It had no place in the life he was making for himself. "I do, Dad. I finally do."

From behind him, he heard Austin say, "If I jumped from the back of the chair, I bet I could take him down."

Emmett added, "It'll take two of us, but wait till Mom leaves the room."

Mason glanced over his shoulder, and both of his brothers smiled at him innocently. He flexed his arms, silently challenging them to bring it on, then winked and turned away from them.

His parents had sent him to enough martial arts classes that he could hold his own against two little ninjas. He heard them whispering and plotting against him and laughed. *I hope.*

Chapter Twenty-One

That Friday night, Chelle sat snuggled up to Mason on the swing on her parents' porch. "Everyone seemed to get along well," she said.

"My favorite part of dinner was when I was asking you to marry me, and my brothers started roughhousing at the table. Your father ended their nonsense with one 'Enough.' Was he a drill sergeant?"

"He was," Chelle said dreamily, enjoying the conversation, but loving the feeling of being in Mason's arms more. "He's a big marshmallow on the inside, but he brings out that voice when he needs to."

"I thought my father was going to fall out of his chair in shock when Emmett and Austin listened to him." He kissed Chelle on the temple. "I never thought I would want children, but I've changed my mind. What do you think of six?"

Six? Chelle sat up in surprise. "Are you serious?"

Mason laughed. "You don't remember the first night we met? That's how many you said I wanted."

Chelle relaxed. "Let's start with one or two and see how it goes."

"We'll need to live in California for at least two years."

Chelle hugged Mason tightly. "I'm okay with wherever as long as we're together."

Mason hugged her just as tightly. "That's exactly how I feel." He nuzzled her cheek and said, "Millie had an idea about a career for you."

"Really?" Chelle asked. "I love Millie. What was it?"

"She thinks you'd be a perfect travel agent. You could help people see the world and have a good excuse to check out all those places yourself. I happen to know someone who is well traveled and would love to show you what he knows."

Chelle pulled his head down near hers and murmured against his lips, "I do like a man with experience."

"You'd better," Mason growled between kisses. "Hey, I didn't buy you a new engagement ring. Did you want one?"

"No." Chelle's voice grew husky. "I love the one I have. If you want to buy me another diamond, I know the perfect shop that has them set in some intriguing devices."

Mason laughed out loud. "I love the way you think."

A few weeks later, Mason and Chelle were in London sipping champagne in a private capsule on the London Eye. They were only there for a long weekend, but the long flight had been worth the look in Chelle's eyes when she'd realized where he'd taken her.

His phone rang. He ignored it at first, but when it continued to ring he checked the number. *Ruby.*

"Who is it?" Chelle asked, not taking her eyes off the view of London's skyline.

Mason hugged her from behind and held out the phone for her to see. "It's Ruby. She's probably contacting me as part of her program."

Chelle leaned into his hug and said, "Answer her."

Mason did. "Ruby."

"Mason, I wanted to say thank you. You didn't have to come when I asked, and I was nasty enough to you that anyone else would have left me. I have no idea why you stayed, but I'm glad you did. I don't know if I can do this, but I'm going to try. I'm going to really try this time."

"I know you can do it, Ruby. Keep telling yourself that you deserve better than the life you have when you're using. And tell yourself that every day. Eventually, you'll start to believe it. That's what happened to me."

Ruby was quiet for a moment. "Are you still with Chelle?"

"I am. We're actually on the London Eye right now."

"Can I speak to her?"

Mason hesitated, then handed the phone to Chelle. He understood now that it didn't matter if Ruby lived up to the person he hoped she was. What mattered was that he trusted his relationship with Chelle to be solid enough in the face of whatever life threw at them. They'd decided to make their life together in California until the end of his term, then decide if they wanted to stay or return to Texas. Either way, he saw himself with Chelle; wherever and however that worked out didn't matter as long as they were together. "Ruby wants to speak to you."

Chelle held the phone to her ear, and Mason heard Ruby explaining how Mason had helped her. She wanted to make sure Chelle wasn't under the impression that there was anything between them. His heart was thudding loudly in his chest as he heard Chelle speak to Ruby warmly, kindly. Chelle had never been more beautiful to him, and he had to blink several times to see the skyline clearly.

Chelle hung up and handed the phone back to Mason. "Ruby said she is halfway through her program. I hope she stays with it."

"Me too," Mason said and kissed Chelle lightly on the head. "Me too."

They stayed like that for a few long moments, then Mason decided to lighten the mood. He reached into his pocket and pulled out a small square box. "I have a present for you."

Chelle turned in his arms and leaned back so she could see his face. "You don't think London was enough? Mason, you don't need to give me more gifts. I have you. That's all I need."

"I owed you this." He couldn't help smiling as he said it.

"Really? Now I'm intrigued." She opened the box between them and picked up the black lace thong and bra with her thumb and finger. "Nice, but underwear? Wait, these look familiar. These look just like the ones I lost in Sacramento."

Mason chuckled and looped his hands behind her back. "I know. I took them."

"What? Why?"

He kissed her lips lightly. "I didn't want anyone else to see you in them."

She shook her head with a smile. "I bought them with you in mind."

"I wasn't sure, and I wasn't taking any chances."

"Mason Thorne, I didn't think you had a jealous bone in your body."

He pulled her closer, crushing the box between them. "Only with you, Chelle." He kissed her again and said, "How long is this ride, anyway? I want to see you in your gift."

Chelle smiled. "Is that all you can think about?"

He grinned and began to whisper some other ideas in her ear. Wicked ideas he knew she'd love.

She laughed and smacked him playfully on the chest. "You're so bad. I love that about you."

Acknowledgments

A special thanks to my editors: Karen Lawson, Janet Hitchcock, Marion Archer, Krista Stroever, and Christopher Werner.

My street team, Ruthie's Roadies, for keeping this journey fun.

My husband, Tony. I couldn't do this without him.

My children for being patient with the crazy schedule writing sometimes demands.

About the Author

Ruth Cardello was born the youngest of eleven children in a small city in northern Rhode Island. She lived in Boston, Paris, Orlando, and New York before coming full circle and moving back to Rhode Island, where she lives with her husband and three children. Before turning her attention to writing, Ruth was an educator for twenty years, eleven of which she spent as a kindergarten teacher. She has written sixteen previous novels, several of which made the *New York Times* and *USA Today* bestseller lists. *Taken Home* is the third book in the Lone Star Burn series.